The Black Bonnet

The Black Bonnet

Louella Bryant

The New England Press, Inc.
Shelburne, Vermont

For Bryant

Manufactured in the United States of America
First Edition
Cover illustration by Kathryn Hewitt

For additional copies of this book or a catalog of our other titles,
please write:
New England Press
P.O. Box 575
Shelburne, VT 05482

Bryant, Louella, 1947-
    The black bonnet / Louella Bryant. -- 1st ed.
        p.   cm.
    Summary: As they near the end of their journey to freedom along the
Underground Railroad, twelve-year-old Charity and her sixteen-
year-old sister Bea encounter additional perils.
    ISBN 1-881535-22-3
    [1. Underground railroad--Fiction. 2. Fugitive slaves--Fiction.
3. Slavery--Fiction. 4. Afro-Americans--Fiction.] I. Title.
PZ7.B8395B1   1996
[Fic]--dc20   96-31672
                                                      CIP
                                                       AC

Contents

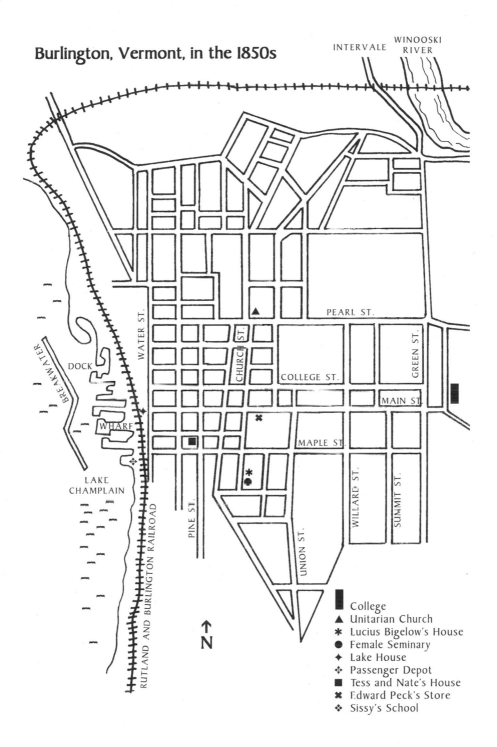

Burlington, Vermont, in the 1850s

INTERVALE

WINOOSKI RIVER

BREAKWATER

DOCK

WATER ST.

CHURCH ST.

PEARL ST.

GREEN ST.

COLLEGE ST.

MAIN ST.

WHARF

MAPLE ST.

LAKE CHAMPLAIN

PINE ST.

WILLARD ST.

SUMMIT ST.

UNION ST.

RUTLAND AND BURLINGTON RAILROAD

↑ N

■ College
▲ Unitarian Church
✳ Lucius Bigelow's House
● Female Seminary
✦ Lake House
❖ Passenger Depot
■ Tess and Nate's House
✖ Edward Peck's Store
❖ Sissy's School

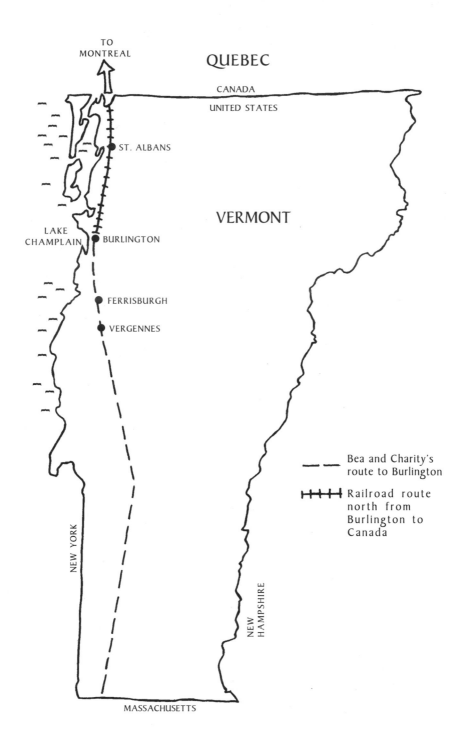

TO
MONTREAL

QUEBEC

CANADA
UNITED STATES

ST. ALBANS

VERMONT

LAKE
CHAMPLAIN   BURLINGTON

FERRISBURGH

VERGENNES

———   Bea and Charity's
route to Burlington

┼┼┼┼   Railroad route
north from
Burlington to
Canada

NEW YORK

NEW
HAMPSHIRE

MASSACHUSETTS

Acknowledgments

Thanks to the librarians in Special Collections at the University of Vermont Bailey/Howe Library and the Fletcher Free Library in Burlington and to the Shelburne Museum for help in researching this novel. *Vermont's Anti-Slavery and Underground Railroad Record* by Wilbur Siebert, *Six Women's Slave Narratives: Incidents in the Life of a Slave Girl* by Harriet Jacobs, and stories by Rowland Robinson were precious resources. Thanks also to Adrienne Capone for reading and criticizing the manuscript and to my husband, Harrison Reynolds, for support and encouragement. And special acknowledgment to my son, Bryant Welch, for writing the seventh grade paper about the underground railroad in Burlington that inspired me to write this novel.

Chapter One

A rifle shot cracked the icy night. Charity collided with the stone-hard back of her sister, who had stopped in midstride.

"Bea, what—?" said Charity.

Bea grabbed Charity's hand and yanked her into the forest beside the railroad tracks. She pushed Charity toward the scabby trunk of a broad pine and pressed against her back. The drill was done with the precision that comes from repetition. They practiced every night. Every sound was a warning to duck out of sight and stay hidden until the way was clear. Sometimes they would wait minutes, sometimes hours. Often it was nothing but a raccoon or a deer, but once in a while someone would ride by. In the dark it was hard to tell why they were out riding at night, and Bea and Charity could take no chances.

"Bea?" said Charity.

"Hush," Bea commanded. Bea was tall enough to rest her chin on top of Charity's head. When her arms came around Charity's, they brought with them the ends of the ragged blanket she wore around her shoulders. Charity buried her hands in the scratchy wool. The heat from Bea's body rose about her, sweet as hay in a barn full of horses.

A dog barked in the distance, and the echo settled into stillness. Charity felt Bea's heart thump like a slow drum beat. They had not been walking fast. They always conserved their energy and stepped along at a steady pace. That way they could cover a greater distance without exhausting themselves.

But walking slow didn't keep Charity's feet from hurting badly. They were wet and aching, and the blisters on her heels were raw. The soles of the old shoes were worn thin, and her toes were worrying the ends. They had once belonged to Bethy, the spoiled daughter of the plantation owner at Primrose in Virginia, where Charity was born and the only place she had ever lived. Bethy was without doubt the product of a momentary truce between her parents, whose bickering was part of the daily routine at the plantation.

Bethy was thirteen, almost a year older than Charity. She was large-boned, but not in the way Bea was. Bea was solid, like the frame of a well-built house, one that could withstand the fiercest storms. But Bethy was gawky. Her arms and legs jutted out at angles, and she moved without much coordination, as if one limb had no idea what the other was doing. She could never thread a needle, which Charity always had to do for her, and her crewel was sloppy and uneven. She often broke things, like the china vase by the foyer mirror, which she knocked with her elbow while putting on her hat. She wore dresses with lace and ruffles that looked silly on her. Riding breeches and boots would have suited her better.

Charity got plenty of hand-me-downs from Bethy, most of which she had left behind in her corner of the Primrose kitchen. The pretty shoes were precious, however, even though they were meant for a white girl's party, not for a black girl tromping through woods for what must have been more than

2

five hundred miles. And who knew how much farther they had to go?

Charity looked up at the Vermont sky, where thousands of tiny lanterns lighted the way. She had kept her eye on the drinking gourd during the past weeks. Bea said its dipper would point them toward the north. She saw it there now, still and silent, as if floating in a black sea. It was something she could count on. The night air was so quiet that she could hear her own breathing. Last night the wind had cut deeply, numbing her hands and feet. She and Bea sneaked into a barn to warm up, and Charity had curled up like a cat, her head against her knees, until she could feel her toes and fingers again.

Everything in this wilderness seemed frozen—the lakes, the ground, and even sound. It was only March, and spring, she had been told, comes late to New England. The border to Canada was closer every day, but in this weather it seemed like a broken promise.

Charity slipped her hand out of Bea's blanket and picked at a piece of bark on the tree. They watched trees carefully, never getting too far from their cover, reading the moss, which always grows on the north side of the trunk. North, where it seemed to get colder and colder each night. If she only had something to eat, it might help. Sundown was hours ago, when they ate a hunk of cheese and a biscuit apiece that Anne Robinson gave them at Rokeby, just outside Ferrisburgh.

She slept in a bed all day at Rokeby, and in late afternoon Anne brought bowls of stew and fresh cornbread. Charity liked Anne, a small woman who talked softly and smelled of spices. Anne might have let them stay another day or two to rest and build up their strength, but before dusk Anne's brother came in with news that a southerner was in Vergennes, the town Bea and Charity passed through the night before. The southerner was looking for a fugitive, a black man in his twen-

3

ties, and he might insist on searching Rokeby. Without a word, Bea began gathering her few things, signaling her decision to move on. Charity knew Bea was saving Anne's last two biscuits for the hours just before dawn to get them through the final miles of the night. They would be hard and cold, and it would take a long time to gnaw them into bits soft enough to swallow.

Charity lay her head back onto her sister's shoulder. The sliver of moon lit the night like candlelight, glinting off the snow that covered the countryside. She could just make out the railroad tracks, two dark streaks cutting a path through the white blanket like an arrow pointing north. The snow was cold and difficult to walk through, but worse, it provided anyone tracking the sisters with an easy trail to follow.

The clap of a gunshot sounded again, farther off this time. The dog's bark was muffled by a safe distance. "Must be hunting possum or coon," Bea said. "Anyway, they're going away." Bea was back on the railroad tracks before Charity could think. When Bea ordered, "Pick up your step," Charity stumbled to catch up. Her shoes crunched into the snow, and her skirt, wilted from many washings, whispered with each step. A wagon ride from Middlebury to Burlington took only a day. On foot through snow, it seemed more like a year. This was the third night, and they hoped to reach Burlington before daybreak.

Charity concentrated on the rhythm of her steps and timed her breathing so that her whole body was in harmony. Her eyes followed a triangle from Bea's back to the ground in front of her to her right, where the east would show the first signs of dawn, and again to Bea's back. Mr. Robinson had said, "Look for the mountain shaped like a camel's hump. When it's to your right, you're almost there. The big lake to your left will guide you into town. Go to the brick church on Pearl Street. Someone there will help you." She repeated the words now as if casting a spell that would pick her up and transport her through the air, dropping her down beside the church. Pearl Street. Brick church. Someone will help you.

Chapter Two

By the time they reached the church, gray wisps of light floated around them like ghosts. Bea found the back door and hunched against the brick wall beside it. Her shoulders heaved, and Charity saw that she was sick. She had been sick many times during the last weeks, and Charity worried about her.

"You all right, Bea?" she asked, and she put her hand on Bea's shoulder. Bea nodded and wiped her mouth with her fingers. Charity didn't know what she would do without Bea. The whole journey was Bea's idea. One crisp night she stole into the Primrose kitchen, shook Charity awake, and nearly dragged her away. Charity had no time to grab more than a shawl, although she would have liked to take one or two of Bethy's books. The awkward white girl irritated her, but she was glad she could sit close by when Bethy was being taught her lessons. She liked best the geography books, especially the ones about Africa with names that rolled off her tongue, like Mozambique, Zambia, Ethiopia. And she liked the adventures of Odysseus and Aeneas. She dreamed about going on an adventure too, but traveling at night in this cold was not what she had in mind.

"We'd better get inside, Bea," said Charity. "It's starting to get light." The back door was unlocked, but it was stuck, and Charity had to use both hands to jerk it loose. Bea was usually the stronger one. She was big for sixteen, but she never slouched to make herself seem smaller. She always held her head high, even when she spoke to the white overseers at Primrose. Many times Charity had seen her stare a white man down. Once when Bea came to the big house to see Charity, a field manager stopped her by the flower garden. Bea stood firm and glared at him. His whip twitched in his hand, but after a few minutes he spat and cursed and turned away.

Charity held the door for Bea and closed it tightly behind them. She felt her way down a flight of stairs to the cellar and found a stove glowing against a far wall. Bea struggled toward the warmth and collapsed to the floor, and Charity could tell from her breathing that she was instantly asleep.

Charity, tired as she was, lay awake and thought about Bea. Bea never told Charity why she chose that night to leave or why she was so frantic to put distance between them and Primrose. They ran for miles down a wooded path, Charity following close behind her sister, and came out on a grassy road where a white man sat waiting atop a wagon. He jumped down and helped the girls into the back, then covered them with burlap sacks. They bumped over rutted roads for hours to the Natural Bridge, where he dropped them beside the road and then turned the wagon back toward Roanoke. Bea never said who he was, and Charity had not yet found the right time to ask her.

Charity didn't remember falling asleep, but she awoke with a start. She sensed then heard the men come down the stairs, men who spoke in low, unthreatening tones.

"Any idea where they came from, Joshua?" a deep voice asked.

"I don't know, Lucius. May be part of that group from Carolina that arrived two days ago. They said there might be more coming." The second voice was more resonant, but the vowels were quick, not drawn out like the breathy twang of Virginians.

"What kind of hell have these people been through to want freedom this badly?"

"I'll get some blankets from the rectory. Tonight we'll move them to my house. Mary won't permit any fugitives in the house, but there's space in the livery. It's best not to tell her, but they can stay a night or two. Then we can get them to St. Albans to catch the train."

"They're both exhausted, Joshua, and it looks like there may be frostbite. God knows what else they may be carrying. I don't think they'll be ready to travel for a couple of weeks."

"They're young, Lucius, and the promise of freedom has been the best elixir for many of the others."

"A night in the livery, and then I'll arrange for them to be moved to the ell. They can stay there as long as I can keep the filthy flesh hunters at bay."

The voices faded away, and Charity opened her eyes. Fatigue pressed down on her like a giant hand, pinning her to the floor. She looked at Bea lying next to her, still as death. Charity put her arm over Bea's shoulders. Bea looked a lot like her father. Her lips were thick cushions, and her nose was broad and strong. But her skin was her most beautiful asset. It was smooth, like stones polished under a running brook. It was the color of the chocolate candies Bethy showed her at Christmastime in the kitchen of the big house. Last Christmas Eve, the night before time for opening presents, Charity stumbled on Bethy crouched in a corner of the kitchen. She was delicately peeling the silver paper from a box tied with a bright red bow. Bethy bribed Charity with a piece of chocolate so she wouldn't tell Bethy's mother. Charity remembered the bittersweet taste and the way it melted on her tongue.

Charity kissed her sister's cheek. Her skin had a salty, sweet taste. It was soft, but the bones were close under the surface, like a silk cloth draped over a hard-backed chair. Her own skin was a pale, sickly color, more like Bethy's than Bea's, and she scorned it unless she could put it to use. Last year when the Pearsons had a Christmas party, sweet smells and laughter wafted into the kitchen where Charity helped Penny, the cook, arrange food on trays. She couldn't resist following Penny as she carried the goodies to the table in the dining room. She was wearing one of Bethy's nicest outgrown dresses, and Penny had woven her braid with the ribbons Charity had hoarded from Bethy's castoffs. She stood for a moment admiring the opulence of the feast in front of her. Silver candelabras cast a soft glow over platters of meat and breads, and rich cakes glistened with frosting. Then she felt a hand on her arm.

"Hello," said a woman she had never seen before. "You must be Bethy's little sister. What's your name?"

Charity stared at her for a moment, then she said, "No ma'am, I'm Char—"

"Sarah, dear," interrupted Miss Priscilla, Bethy's mother. "Come meet Lieutenant Brigham. He's a West Point graduate—and he's not married!" She glared over her shoulder at Charity as she ushered the woman into the parlor. Charity knew then that she had a secret weapon and filed it into her memory.

It came in handy again on their trip north when she and Bea missed the landmark for the next safe house. They finally stopped at a weathered saltbox. Neither girl could have walked much farther that night, and daylight was about to break over the hilltops. Charity pushed her shoulders back, lifted her chin, and marched up to the front door.

"Where are you going?" Bea said fiercely.

"Just stay back a little way and don't say anything," said Charity, and she knocked on the door. A woman answered. Her gray hair was pulled back into a neat bun, and her face was pleasant. "My girl and I are on our way to meet my parents in the next town," Charity said. "We've been visiting my cousin who lives about ten miles back, and he was driving us to the meeting place when his horse went lame. We've been walking nearly all night. We must be lost, and we're about to drop. You wouldn't happen to have a place where we could rest awhile, do you?" The woman raised her eyebrows and put her fists on her hips.

"Well, a young girl like you has no business being out at night like this," she said. "Come on in and I'll see if I can scare up some food. Your folks must be worried sick. Bring her in, too," she said, gesturing toward Bea. Charity flashed a grin at her sister. She enjoyed her supper that night with particular relish.

Charity had worked in the big house since she was five, when Master Pearson, Bethy's father, brought her from the slave quarters to be Bethy's companion. She knew it was easy compared with field work, but she missed Bea and the other children in the slave quarters. She was rarely allowed to leave the kitchen except to pick herbs for Penny. Sunday was the day she looked forward to all week. On Sunday mornings, after Bible readings and a late breakfast at the big house, she was allowed to visit the other slaves for a few hours. There she saw her mother, her father, and Bea. They had worship services until dinner time. Brother James usually did the preaching, which was punctuated with affirmations from his appreciative congregation. It was only on Sundays, when the white drivers were away, that they dared to speak of freedom. "I am bound for the Promised Land," they sang, the deep baritones of the men's voices anchoring the mellow altos of the women. "I am bound for the Promised Land. Oh, who will come and go with me? I am bound for the Promised Land." After the service came the hugging and handshaking and asking after each other's health. Charity was always greeted like a lost child returned home after a long time away, even though it had only been a week.

After dinner Charity sat cross-legged in front of her mother, Annie, on the dirt floor of the shed where her mother and father slept. She watched the evening sun send spears of pink and yellow light through the chinks between the boards while her mother combed the tangles from her hair. It was long and thick and would hang in her eyes if allowed to. Her mother's hands were large and rough, but they darted through the clumps of hair like delicate birds weaving a nest. When she was finished, the braid was so tight that tears often ran down Charity's cheeks. Once she protested, but Annie said it had to be tight to stay that way until next Sunday. Bethy told her she looked more like an Indian than a Negro, and when Charity threatened to scalp her, Bethy ran directly to her mother. That night Charity endured the sting of Miss Priscilla's switch.

She loved the woolly feel of Bea's hair, which was like her father's. Her mother's head was always wrapped in a cloth, turban-style, and Charity could not remember ever seeing her without it.

Before Charity left to go back to the big house on Sunday evenings, Annie would give her instructions for the week. "Don't talk back to white folks. Do what they tell you, and don't waste time about it," she would say. "You be happy you're at the big house instead of out here in the burning sun working your fingers to the bone." Each week she ended her lecture the same way. "Some day you'll be free, honey, and won't nobody be telling you what to do but yourself."

And then Annie was gone. Bethy said she was sold to a landowner in Richmond. She said her mother and father had argued about Annie for as long as she could remember. It was Bethy's mother who wanted Annie sent away, and her father finally gave in to get some peace. Charity never knew what her mother had done to upset Miss Priscilla. She couldn't remember them ever talking to each other except once, when she was very young and had not been at the big house very long. Annie came to see her on her sixth birthday carrying a little cake on an earthenware plate. She had made it out of cornmeal and molasses, and decorated it with peanuts and wild strawberries. Miss Priscilla was in the kitchen checking on supper when Annie knocked at the back door.

"What do you want?" Miss Priscilla snapped.

"It's my daughter's birthday," said Annie. "I've brought her something."

Miss Priscilla's eyebrows arched into sharp angles. "Slaves do not celebrate birthdays at Primrose," she yelled. "Especially the daughter of a whore." She slapped Annie's face, and the cake fell from Annie's hands and splattered onto the floor. The plate broke into pieces and clattered across the kitchen. "Now get out," hissed Miss Priscilla. Annie looked at her daughter. Her eyes held Charity in a momentary embrace. Then she lifted her chin, set her jaw, and looked down at Miss Priscilla, who was half a head shorter than Annie. She turned without saying anything and walked away, leaving the birthday cake in messy lumps at Charity's feet.

"Clean it up," demanded Miss Priscilla. Charity did as she was told, but her own face stung with indignation.

Her mother never came to the big house again. And her father, although he doted on Bea, had only harsh words for

Charity or ignored her altogether. His angry outbursts frightened her. After her mother was taken away, Charity began to dread Sundays, except for seeing Bea, and made excuses to go back early to the big house, where she sat alone in the kitchen and read books until Penny returned from her visits to the slave quarters.

Penny was a plump woman who liked generous samples of her own cooking. She had never had children and was not fond of others', but she took over the task of combing and braiding Charity's hair when Charity asked her to. She was not very good at it though, and tendrils would spring loose hours afterward. By the week's end, Bethy would refer to her hair as "the mop," and Charity began tying it into a cloth, much as her mother had done.

Bea stirred, and Charity realized they were alone in the church cellar. The two men had gone. Charity was surprised to see that they had both been covered with blankets. The mats between them and the floor were not as soft as the straw beds in the barns where they had slept in the past weeks. Charity sat up. The ceiling was low with stone posts supporting it. One high window was coated with frost, but some light found its way into the room. On a table against a wall was a pitcher filled with water, a bowl for washing, and some cloths. Next to them was a loaf of bread and a jar of jam. Charity left the washing for later and reached to satisfy her growling stomach.

Chapter Three

❦

The sisters slept all day. As night fell again, Charity suddenly came out of a deep sleep. She didn't hear the man come down the stairs or swing open the door, but she opened her eyes when she sensed his presence. Not that he was impressive-looking. He was no taller than Bea, skinny as a broom handle, and about as straight. His face was smooth, and his fair hair was combed back, sticking tightly to his head. His eyes turned down slightly at the corners, and his thin lips were pursed firmly together. He cleared his throat before he spoke. "My name is Reverend Joshua Young. Welcome to Burlington."

Charity recognized the voice as one of the two she had heard when they first arrived. She didn't answer. Bea stared blankly at him.

"You don't have to be afraid," he said. She wasn't, but he must have mistaken Charity's lack of enthusiasm for trepidation. "Fugitives come through town every day. You'll be safe until you're both ready to travel again. Then we'll see you on

14

your way to the border." He hesitated a minute then ran his index finger down the top of his thin nose, and his mouth threatened a smile. "And don't worry—we haven't lost anyone yet."

Charity spoke before she had time to weigh her words. "What do you mean, 'yet?' Are you expecting to lose someone?"

He blinked at Charity as if her question surprised him, then a frown clouded his face. "We can't be too careful. Slavery turns men into villains. Have you heard of the Fugitive Slave Law?" Of course she had. All the slaves knew about this law. It began before she came to the big house and now, in 1858, it was still a threat to any slaves running away from their owners. She knew that if she and Bea were caught by a slave catcher—any slave catcher—he could claim them as his own property, and they could not say anything to contradict him. Master Pearson's men weren't the only ones that they had to fear. Anyone with a greedy disposition could sell them and pocket the money. They had to be wary, even of ministers.

"They're not going to catch us. We'll die first." It was Bea who spoke now. Charity turned to look at her. She had never thought she might die. Life at Primrose was all she knew, and, except for the beatings, it didn't seem that bad to her.

"Forgive me," he said. "You must have come a long way. After you've rested a while, you'll feel better. And you'll need some warmer clothes. Canada is even colder than it is here. My house is a short way up Pearl Street. The stable will have to do for tonight, but when Mr. Bigelow has made the arrangements, he'll take you both to his house, where you'll be more comfortable."

"Who's Mr. Bigelow?" said Charity.

"He owns the local newspaper. Next to the mayor, he's the most respected man in town. You can trust him." He pulled the collar of his coat up around his neck. "But we should go now, while it's dark. We can't risk your being seen in daylight. Strangers come into town nearly every hour, and most of them have their noses to the ground." He motioned toward the door, and Charity made a move to gather their things.

"Oh, one more thing," said Reverend Young. "A man named Hendrick stopped by the rectory yesterday asking about two Negro girls from Virginia. Do you know him?"

"No, I don't think—" began Charity.

"Yes, I know him," said Bea. Strength seemed to surge back into her limp limbs, and she raised herself up off her pallet. "But I wouldn't call him a man. Devil is more like it." Her voice simmered with contempt.

"But, who . . . ?" Charity broke off.

"He works for Master Pearson. Lives in a shed near the slave quarters so he can keep an eye on us day and night." She looked at Reverend Young. "How much farther to the border? Can we make it tonight?"

"No, no," said Reverend Young. "It's impossible to walk that far in a day, and it's too risky to put you on a train without making the proper connections. Besides, you're in no shape to travel for a few days." Bea slumped back onto the blanket.

Charity had never heard of this man Hendrick. She knew Master Pearson had many men who worked for him, and men came and went often from Primrose. Maybe if she had spent less time with her face in a book she would know more about what went on around her.

"We should go now," said Reverend Young. Charity focused what was left of her energy on willing her body to move one more time.

Chapter Four

Charity's sleep in the tack room of the livery was deep and dreamless. When she awoke, eyes as green as pond water stared into her own. They floated in a cherubic face the color of fresh cream. The stubby nose was sprinkled with freckles, and a pink tongue searched the corners of the mouth. The whole visage was framed with a mass of fiery waves, and Charity could feel the warmth emanating from her closeness. "Are you awake?" the mouth yelled at her, even though it was only inches away.

"I'm awake, but I'm not deaf," said Charity.

"Well, I've got something for you." The lips flattened across the teeth into a grin.

Charity sat up. The girl's orange hair flamed out from under her gray bonnet. The short red jacket that was buttoned up under her chin clashed with her hair color. The green skirt did not quite reach her ankles, and the lace trim on her pantalets hung down below the hem. Her heavy boots, tied with leather laces, were caked with mud and snow. She looked a little like last December's Christmas tree in the big house at

Primrose. Charity thought she must be about Bethy's age, but she was very different from Bethy, whose long blonde hair was always combed neatly and tied with fancy ribbons, and whose pastel-colored dresses were always freshly ironed, usually by Charity herself. The girl shoved a bundle toward her.

"Here are some clothes for you. They're from Edward Peck's store. Mr. Bigelow sent them, and my father asked me to bring them over and give them to you. I hope they fit. Father said one of you was big, and the other was just skin and bones. Your friend must be the big one," she said, pushing another bundle at Bea, who was also awakened by the girl's chatter.

"That's my sister," said Charity.

"Well, I wouldn't have guessed that. You sure don't look much alike. I'm Cecilia Montgomery Young. You met my father last night. He's the preacher at the Unitarian Church. Some say he's as good as Mr. Emerson himself, and he's the greatest Unitarian minister alive. He lives in Massachusetts, and they say he can preach Satan out of a whore."

"What did you say?" asked Charity, blinking at her. There was that word, the one Miss Priscilla called her mother. Whatever it meant, Charity was sure it wasn't a compliment.

The girl ignored her question. "You can call me Sissy if you like," she said. "Most everyone around here does. You got a name?"

"Charity."

"Charity what?"

"Well, I guess it would be Charity Pearson. That was my master's family name. But if I'm going to be free, I'll be giving myself a brand new name."

"You can have my name. If I'm going to be Young all my life, I'll never get grown up," said Sissy, and she laughed at her own joke. Charity giggled. She was beginning to like this girl. "What's your name?" Sissy asked Bea.

18

"Her name is Bea," said Charity.

"Can't she say her own name?" asked Sissy.

"She doesn't talk much," said Charity.

"My sister doesn't give me much chance to talk," said Bea. "She says enough for both of us."

"Bea's as deep as a slow-moving river. Doesn't look like much is happening on the surface, but there's a lot going on underneath. I don't even know what she's thinking half the time," said Charity.

"Maybe she's not thinking anything," said Sissy.

"I wouldn't count on that. Bea got us all the way from Virginia. She was in a big hurry to leave Primrose. She barely stopped to let me catch my breath these past weeks we've been traveling. I didn't even say good-bye to Bethy. She's Master Pearson's daughter, and I've been waiting on her almost since I can remember. Maybe you could get me some writing paper so I could start a letter. I'll mail it as soon as we reach Canada," said Charity.

"Don't be silly," Sissy laughed. "Slaves can't write. You can't even read. It's against the law."

"Well, it's hard to be around learning all the time and not pick it up," said Charity. "I can read Latin and a little Greek, too. You have anything you'd like me to read for you?"

Sissy pulled a small Bible out of her coat pocket. "Here. Read me something from this."

Charity opened the front cover. "The Holy Bible. Containing the Old and New Testaments. Translated from the original tongues being the version set forth AD 1611."

"Not that part. Start with Genesis," said Sissy.

Charity complied. "In the beginning God created the heavens and the earth. The earth was without form and void, and darkness was upon the face of the deep; and the Spirit of God was moving over the face of the waters. And God said, 'Let there be light'; and there was light. And God saw that the light was good; and God separated the light from the darkness." Charity asked, "Is that enough?"

"How do I know you aren't just reciting that from memory?" asked Sissy.

"Because I can tell you what it means, too," said Charity, and she continued before Sissy had a chance to interrupt. "It says that darkness was around before light, which really means that black people were around before white people. And if we've been around longer than you, blacks should own the plantations and whites should be doing the hard work." Charity had always enjoyed squabbles like this with Bethy. She always ended up sending Bethy into a spin of confusion, which gave Charity great satisfaction, even though it meant bearing the lash before the night was over. It was a small price to pay for flustering the white girl.

"You're bending it all around. It doesn't say that at all," protested Sissy. "Anyway, you're hardly black. You're one of the palest Negroes I've ever seen. Why isn't your skin the color of your sister's?"

"I guess God just ran short of coloration when he got to me," said Charity. "Looks like he plum gave up when he got to you, except for the splatters on your nose."

"You are the most ungracious person I've ever met, Miss Charity whatever-you-decide-your-name-will-be. I could very well take you out on the street and sell you this minute, you know," said Sissy, playfully.

"You wouldn't get much. I'm hardly worth my weight. My skin is too light, my hair is too straight, I'm literate, and I don't know the first thing about planting and harvesting. It's Bea who would draw a bag full of silver. If she had as much money as she's worth, we'd be rich and riding our own railroad car to Canada." They both laughed at the absurdity of Charity's proposition.

"Stop it, both of you," said Bea. "Slavery is nothing to laugh at."

Bea's tone silenced Sissy and Charity.

"I've heard hungry babies crying because their mothers did not dare to stop picking cotton to feed them or they'd get the lash. I've seen men tied to a post and beaten because they weren't working hard enough in the hot sun. The whip opens old scars from other beatings. Sometimes days pass before they're cut loose. I've tended the wounds, swollen and infected, sometimes squirming with maggots. I've heard the cries of women whose husbands were sent to the slave market. Our own mother was sold away. We don't know where she is, and we most likely won't ever see her again."

Bea was sitting up, her hands clenching her knees.

"Freedom is still a long way away, sister, and danger is everywhere." Bea's eyes flashed like swords then slowly closed. She lay back on her cot.

Charity looked at Sissy, who was studying a piece of straw caught in her skirt. Neither girl spoke for a minute. Bea was right—slavery wasn't something to joke about, least of all with a white girl.

The livery door creaked open, and a strange man nearly filled the doorway. His fine wool clothes were as nice as any Master Pearson ever wore. The whiskers on the sides of his face were flecked with silver. Bushy eyebrows shaded his pale blue eyes. He reached up and took his top hat by the brim, then placed it gently under his arm.

"Hello, Mr. Bigelow," said Sissy.

"Good evening, Cecilia. I see you've taken good care of our visitors," said Mr. Bigelow.

21

"Yes, sir. They're from Virginia. This is Charity, and her sister, Bea," said Sissy.

"I'm very pleased to meet you," he said, bowing slightly. "My name is Lucius Bigelow. You're welcome to stay in my home until your strength has returned. You will be given whatever you need. But you may have to share your accommodations with the others, if you don't mind."

"Others?" Charity frowned.

"Every week as many as twenty find their way to Burlington for a night or more until we can send them north to Montreal. I give you my word that I'll do everything I can to ensure your safety while you're here." He did not wait for an answer. "And now, it's almost daybreak. Cecilia, will you help? My wagon is outside, but my house is not far."

Sissy let Bea use her shoulder for support. The circulation had brought Charity's feet back to life, and they stung as if needles were sticking into them. Her whole body was stiff and sore, and every part hurt. She thought about Montreal. It wouldn't be long now.

Chapter Five

Mr. Bigelow's wagon had a false bottom with a hidden compartment under it. Charity and Bea crawled in and wrapped heavy blankets around themselves, but not even the thick batting could keep out the bitter, predawn chill. Charity was tired of the snow and freezing rain that constantly threatened. She missed the misty mornings of Virginia and the warm sunshine that followed, even in the winter. Here the cold burned her nostrils. Although the thick smell of wood smoke from chimneys hung over the whole town, it provided no heat. She also missed Bethy's books. Reading was as natural to her as breathing. She had had to remember to keep Bethy from knowing how much she loved literature or how much better she could read than Bethy, or the books would have been ripped from her hands. When they read aloud, Charity would stumble over words that she knew well so Bethy could correct her. For these pretenses, she was sometimes rewarded by being allowed to take a book to the kitchen at night.

"To practice," Bethy said. She would stay up late straining her eyes by the light of the dying fire.

The horses stopped at a white house. Mr. Bigelow helped Charity and Bea out of the wagon and led them to the back of the house. Sissy was carrying a lantern, which she set down by the narrow door. The handle clanked when she let it go, and Charity looked around to see if anyone else was up at that hour and might have heard. There was a heavy fog, and she could see no one else stirring. Mr. Bigelow pulled a key from his coat pocket, slipped it into the lock, and turned it. Inside they climbed a steep, narrow flight of stairs to an attic. Sissy put the lantern on a small stand by the door. The roof sloped down to the floor on both sides, but there was plenty of head-room. On the wall at the far end of the room was a window covered with a thick curtain. A potbelly stove stood in the center of the room, and wooden chairs sat by it. Several beds made up neatly with colorful quilts lined the perimeter. Mr. Bigelow told Charity and Bea to make themselves comfortable, and that food would be brought to them three times a day. If they needed anything, they could ask for it at mealtimes.

"And one more thing," he said. "Never pull back the window curtain. Word is about regarding the presence of fugitives in this house. Slave hunters frequent the railroad station, only a few blocks away. It is best to be prudent." Bea shuddered and fell onto a chair. Mr. Bigelow pointed out a box of medical supplies, and then he left.

"I'll be going, too," said Sissy. "I go to school today, but I'll come back this evening for a visit."

"Does that school give you books?" asked Charity.

"Of course," said Sissy. "I'll bring you some if you think there's anything you haven't read," she teased.

Charity helped Bea to a bed and covered her with a quilt. Then she sat down and took off her shoes. Her feet still hurt, and she rubbed them. A pot of water was steaming on the stove. The sun was coming up, she guessed, because light struggled dimly through the window curtain. She couldn't remember the last time she had watched the sun rise and felt its warmth seep into her skin. She had become a nocturnal creature, flying on batlike instinct.

A movement caught her eye on one of the beds in a corner of the room. A mound of covers moved again, and then it coughed. Charity jumped to her feet and walked cautiously toward the bed. She pulled the covers back slowly. It was a woman. A red cloth was tied around her head, and her hair, woven with white strands, stuck up behind it like a dark halo. She rubbed her eyes with her fingertips. Half of the last finger on her left hand was missing, and the others were rough and knobby. Her hands were marked with scars and looked like they had seen years of hard work.

Charity stepped closer. She had not seen another fugitive the entire trip from Virginia.

"Well," the woman said, "looks like the Lord done sent two more pilgrims on the road to Paradise."

"I'm Charity. And this is my sister, Bea."

"Name's Sunday. Named after the day I was born." She smiled, revealing a gap between her two front teeth. Her tawny skin was stretched tightly over her high cheekbones, and, except for two vertical lines between her eyebrows, her face had no wrinkles. At first Charity thought she was a young woman, but her dark eyes were tired and haunted.

"My mother always said being born on Sunday was a good sign, but Lord knows I've seen a heap of troubles in the forty-some years I've been on this earth," she said. "I've lost five children to slavery. All of them sold off. I would have sent them to the Lord with my own hands instead of having them be slaves. But those white demons tore them right out of my arms. I gave them my blood and my milk, and the man says they don't belong to me. Ain't enough silver in the world to pay for what my babies was worth to me." She stopped, and her eyes followed the line of the stovepipe to where it disappeared through the ceiling. Then she spoke again. "At least their daddy's found peace."

"Is he free?" said Charity.

"His soul is. His body's laying at the bottom of a grave with a bullet in its back. He was going up north to get a job, save every cent till he could come back and buy me and the children. He never set foot outside Tennessee. I sure hope he's watching over them. I know he's watching over me. One night I just tied some things in a rag and walked off. Walked almost the whole way from Tennessee and never looked back. Didn't want to turn into no pillar of salt. I've poured out enough salt in tears and sweat already. My sweet honey years gotta be in front of me now. But listen to me rattle on. You children must be worn out. Sit down here and let me look at your feet."

Charity sat on the edge of the bed, and Sunday pulled her feet up to inspect them. "How long have you been here?" asked Charity.

"A little more than two weeks. I was about dead when I got here. Mr. Bigelow found me outside the train station and brought me here. I don't remember much except I was determined to get myself on a northbound train. I don't think I would have made it to Canada in one piece. Mrs. Bigelow's been doctoring me so good I'll be able to move on in another day or two. You'll be fine, too. Just need to stay off these feet for a while." Charity winced when Sunday rubbed her big toes.

"Your sister looks like she's in worse shape than you. A woman in her condition shouldn't be making no long trip like this. Still, I guess you got to move when the time's right." Charity was not sure what Sunday meant about Bea's condition, but she kept quiet.

"You rest a bit, honey," said Sunday, "and then I'll take you down to see the men folks."

"What men?" asked Charity.

"Down in the cellar. That's where they stay. We can get down to see them by the back stairs without going outside. They'll be a big comfort to you. You'll see."

Slowly Charity began to feel warmth returning to her body.

Chapter Six

Chimes from a clock outside marked the passing of each hour. It was a distinguished sound, clear and mellow, reverberating down the slope of Church Street to the ell. By the time they had rung three times that afternoon, Charity was feeling stronger. Short rests seemed to revive her, or maybe she was just used to being tired. Bea was on the bed next to Charity's. She was sound asleep, her lips puffing out with every exhalation. She didn't even move when Charity pulled the quilt up under her chin.

"Best let her sleep," said Sunday.

"I think she might be sick," Charity said.

"Nothing a little time won't take care of. And some good food. I'm a little hungry myself. They got a kitchen downstairs. Come on. Let's go see what's on the fire."

Charity couldn't put up an argument when it came to food. She followed Sunday to the stairs, but then she stopped and turned to look at Bea. She hadn't been separated from her sister since the trip began. Bea was all she had now.

"She's all right," said Sunday. She took Charity's hand and led her down the stairs.

The main floor, Sunday said, just below the attic room, was the library, where Mr. Bigelow read in the evenings. Otherwise, it was rarely used. There was no door from the stairway to the library, so it was safely concealed. At the bottom of the stairs was the door leading outside, but Charity could not see a way into the cellar. Sunday squeezed herself into a small, dark alcove behind the stairs and yelled at the wall as if it could hear. "Y'all got some visitors."

"Who is it?" came a man's voice from behind the wall.

"Sunday. And I've got a friend with me."

Slowly a panel slid sideways, and light from an oil lamp fell into the alcove. A round face looked through the opening. His brow was furrowed over eyes glazed with amber, but his mouth formed a thick smile. A gray beard, neatly trimmed, contrasted with his dark skin like the snow at midnight. His high forehead curved back to wisps of hair. In his right earlobe was a small blue stone that glowed with a strange iridescence.

"Sunday," he acknowledged. "Come right on in." A slow laugh rumbled from his generous belly. His shirt was aged to pale gold, and over it he wore a brown woolen vest, rumpled from wearing. He rubbed his hands down the front of the vest as if to iron out the wrinkles. Then he bowed slightly and extended his right arm, gesturing for them to enter.

"This is Charity, Isaac. Her sister Bea's upstairs. She's got some mending to do before they can go on," said Sunday.

"I trust you and your sister have found some comfort here, Charity?" he asked.

"Yes" was all she could manage to say.

The cellar smelled vaguely of stale cigars and old, damp paper. The walls were built of varying size stones, and two small windows up high let in light, although the heavy glass did not allow objects outside to be seen distinctly. On the wall behind Isaac a blanket, woven from colorful yarn scraps, was nailed into the stones near the overhead beams. Below it was a ledge a foot higher than the floor, on which sat a young boy, no more than seven. He was fidgeting nervously. "This little friend is George Washington Henderson. George was brought here by Moses herself," said Isaac, proudly.

Charity's mouth fell open. "You mean Harriet Tubman?" She had heard stories about the black woman who risked her life to guide slaves to the free states. They talked often about her on Sundays at Primrose. Charity thought she was more myth than reality.

"The same," said Isaac. "The virtual spirit of the underground railroad. Last I heard, the price on her head was $40,000, enough for a man to live on without ever working another day of his life. Those Southerners must be awfully desperate to want a scrawny woman that bad. That makes George a celebrity . . . by association." George squirmed. Like most children, he looked like he had trouble sitting still.

"What is she like, George?" asked Charity.

"She's got a gun," said George, the words almost exploding from him. His eyebrows arched as he spoke. "And she'd use it, too. She almost shot a man one night. He was scared, and he tried to run back to his master. She told him, 'Dead Negroes tell no tales.' He came along with us after all." He sucked in a quick breath and kept talking, his words tripping over each other to get out.

"She carried me sometimes when I got real tired and just couldn't walk another step. She could carry a grown man, too. I never saw a woman strong as Moses. And when we'd be resting, she'd sing us a song or tell us a story. Sometimes she'd kind of fall asleep in the middle of it for a minute, then she'd wake up and start right back up where she left off."

30

Isaac interrupted. "They say she suffered a blow to the head with a metal pipe when she was a young slave. Since then she loses consciousness occasionally. But it never keeps her from leading us to freedom."

"What will happen to George?" asked Charity.

"I'll see to it that he gets to Canada, but I'll have to find a family to take him in," said Isaac. "George, I'm afraid, is an orphan. I'd adopt him myself, but I'll be trying to find my way back to Europe."

"You mean you've been there before?" said Charity.

"Um-hum. I made several trips there with Master Southwick—England, Spain, France, Italy. An Algerian in southern France gave me this sapphire," he said, touching his ear. "It was during a long stay in London that I learned to read and write. In fact, I joined a Masonic lodge there and enjoyed the fraternity of black brothers."

"Why would you want to run away from all that?" asked Charity.

"Master Southwick died. His will said I was to be set free. I was living in a little place near the plantation, and one day some slave catchers came and put the chains on me."

"But you were free. It was illegal," said Charity.

"Nothing's legal for a black man anywhere in the south. They didn't waste any time getting me up on the auction block, either. Only thing that saved me was the sign of the Masonic order." He held up his hand. "A fellow mason helped me escape. Now I intend to have the freedom that is rightfully mine."

He stuck his thumbs in the armholes of his vest and rocked back onto his heels. "Well, now. Enough about me. How about a little sustenance? Sunday's always got a good appetite. I'll bet you do, too."

"Yes, sir," said Charity. He led them to a wooden table and

dished some beans onto plates from a kettle hanging in the fireplace.

"Hungry, George?" asked Isaac.

"Naw," he said, "'less you got some of that bread left I can put some syrup on."

"Sure." Isaac took a hunk of bread from a metal box and brought it, with a tin can, to the table. Drops of sticky brown liquid had dripped down the sides. "George has developed a taste for the Yankees' maple syrup." George jumped from his seat, and the blanket swayed behind him.

"Why do you have a blanket hanging on the wall?" Charity asked.

"The fugitives before us have been busy, Charity, and behind that woolen curtain is the fruit of their labors," said Isaac.

"Can I show her?" asked George. Isaac nodded, and George lifted the curtain.

Charity could hardly believe her eyes. A gaping hole had been chiseled right through the wall. It was almost large enough for George to stand in, and, with the light in the room, it extended as far as Charity could see.

"What . . .?" Charity said. George took the lantern from the table and crawled into the opening. Charity saw that it was a tunnel leading from the cellar room. "Where does it go?" she managed to say.

"It connects with the cellar of the Female Seminary next door. It's a school for young white women. The man who owns it, Mr. Converse, is the principal of the school. Mr. Bigelow's house is watched by police and slave hunters, but no one expects fugitives to hide in a school for girls. Just last night two friends crawled through the passage. Mr. Bigelow met them at the seminary and drove them north to St. Albans, where he put them on a train for Canada. By now, they are singing the songs of freedom."

Charity bit her lip. "We don't have any money for a train ticket," she said.

"Don't worry about that," said Isaac. "Mr. Bigelow is a generous man. Your ticket will be paid for, and you'll even find coins in your pocket when you board the train."

Charity's head began to spin. Emotions swirled around her like dust in a room that has just been swept. Her life at Primrose was all she had ever known, and she had accepted it passively. Now she was ashamed of her complacency. She was angry and homesick when she looked back, and hopeful and grateful when she looked forward. Suddenly she felt hot, and a watery veil closed between her and the room. Her lips were damp. She pressed the back of her hand to each nostril and sniffed.

"Isaac," said Sunday, "the child needs to rest. All this business is too much for her to take in at one time. Besides, I still got to prepare her for what she don't know about her sister."

Chapter Seven

Wagons rattled by outside the attic window, and bells jingled. The sun through the curtain coated the room with a honey glow. Charity must have slept all evening and through the night. Bea and Sunday were still asleep. She swung her feet over the side of the bed and knocked over a pile of books. Sissy had apparently left them for her last night. She was surprised that she had not awakened when Sissy came in. The young white girl did not tread with delicate feet.

The morning was chilly, and Charity brought the books onto the bed and covered her legs. There were four volumes. She read each title slowly to draw out the pleasure of discovery. *The Merchant of Venice.* She had read several of Shakespeare's plays, but not this one. *Evangeline.* Although she had seen Henry Wadsworth Longfellow's poems in Bethy's collections, she had not seen this epic. Poems by William Cullen Bryant she would use to fill in between books. *Last of the Mohicans* by James Fenimore Cooper she had already read. She put it aside to read again if she finished the others. It was a good collection, she thought, and the books would help pass the time until Bea was well enough to leave.

At the bottom of the pile was a newspaper called *The Liberator*. The light in the room was not enough to read the fine print, so, without thinking, Charity slipped out of bed and went to the window. She pulled back the curtain and stood, letting the daylight pour in on her. It was as delicious as syrup over oatmeal. When her eyes adjusted to the brightness, she looked down and saw what must have been the Bigelow's side yard. Beyond the splotches of crusty snow and puddles of mud was a driveway with rutted wagon tracks leading from the road to a carriage house behind some leafless trees. Next to the driveway stood a mammoth building whose bricks had been painted a bright yellow. It had at least a dozen chimneys, and most of them were spouting smoke into a clear blue sky. The columns supporting the front porch and all the trim were painted white, and it looked like it was dressed up for a party. It was the Female Seminary. Charity looked at the driveway again and realized that the tunnel she had seen last night was there under that very ground, and her heart began to race.

A man was coming down the steps of the school with a leather bag on his back. He had some letters in his hand. He was breathing hard, and Charity could see the clouds his breath left hanging in the air. As he descended the last step, he turned and started walking toward the ell. His eyes slowly moved upward. Charity was paralyzed. When his eyes met hers, he stopped in midstride.

"What are you doing at that window, child? Didn't Mr. Bigelow tell you not to lift that curtain?" Sunday grabbed Charity's arm and yanked her away from the window. The curtain dropped back down over the glass.

"Did anybody see you out there? I don't know what I'm gonna do with you. You'll get us all sent back to purgatory."

Sunday led her back to her bed and sat her down, then stood with her arms crossed over her breasts.

"No," said Charity.

"No, what?" demanded Sunday.

"I didn't see anyone. I mean, no one saw me. Just the post-man."

"Just the postman? He was white, wasn't he?"

"Well, yes, but I think it's all right. I don't think he really saw me."

Bea was awake by then and asked what was going on. "Your little sister just about gave us all away, looking out that win-dow," said Sunday. She was practically raving now. "You see this hand?" She held up the hand with four fingers. "You know what happened to this finger? I'll tell you. I took a piece of suet from the smokehouse to flavor the soup for my children. But I'm lucky. It could have been my whole hand. You think about that, child." She turned and jammed some wood into the stove, mumbling to herself about how people so small could be such big fools.

"I'm sorry," said Charity.

"Just a little while longer, sister," said Bea. "Then you can take a bath in all the sunshine you like. Just a little longer."

Charity sat silently for a moment and then picked up *The Liberator* again. She held it close to her face so she could read it in the dim light. A man named William Lloyd Garrison was the publisher, and all the stories were about abolition. One article told about Sojourner Truth, the old black woman who agitated the white man's conscience. America, she said, owes a debt to the Negro people, and her strong voice pres-sured the Congress to begin repaying it by repealing the Fugi-tive Slave Law and outlawing slavery. Another article said that a man named Abe Lincoln was running for the Illinois Senate. Although his chances of defeating Senator Stephen

Douglas were slim, his speeches against the atrocities of slavery made people take notice. Charity was especially interested in a story about John Brown, a white man who advocated an armed rebellion against slave owners, as the slave preacher Nat Turner had tried twenty-five years earlier. If they wouldn't listen to reason, said Brown, they would have to listen to guns. The Northerners seemed serious enough about ending slavery to fight about it. Charity wondered if it would come to that and if she would some day be able to return to the old hills of Virginia.

The door opened, and Mrs. Bigelow entered, carrying breakfast. She was a neat woman with wheat-colored hair tied back with a ribbon and an easy smile. Today, however, the smile was gone, and in its place was a tight line of concern.

"Jim Raskin just brought the mail," she said. "He saw two women at the window this morning, and he was sure that at least one of them was a Negro." Charity's heart pounded in her chest. The room was so quiet that she was sure everyone else could hear it. "I invited him to come in and have a cup of coffee. He said he suspects that Mr. Bigelow and I are harboring fugitives here." She put the breakfast tray on a table. "We're lucky, though. He allows the town to think he is neutral, but he told me that he believes slave catching is immoral. He said he won't report us—and I don't think he will—but I don't like having to trust his discretion." She turned toward the door but then stopped. "Please, be more careful. If you're found out, you'll be sent back to your plantations or to worse places, and Mr. Bigelow and I will lose everything—all our possessions, our home—all . . ." Something cut her voice off, and she couldn't finish. She left coffee and oatmeal, but Charity didn't feel like eating much that morning.

She buried her thoughts in *Evangeline*, a long poem about an Acadian girl whose family was forced by the British to leave their home in Nova Scotia. Her lips formed the words at the end of the prelude:

Ye who believe in affection that hopes, and endures, and is patient, Ye who believe in the beauty and strength of a woman's devotion, List to the mournful tradition still sung by the pines of the forest; List to a Tale of Love in Acadie, home of the happy.

She wondered if she would ever have a happy home, a home filled with love. She looked up from the book when she heard clomping on the stairs. Sissy's flaming hair preceded her into the room.

"I guess Christmas came in March, didn't it?" Sissy beamed. The room brightened, and the smell of fresh air emanated from her.

"Why aren't you in school?" asked Charity. She knew she should have thanked Sissy for the books, but Sojourner Truth's words echoed in her head. She refused to feel she was in this white girl's debt.

"It's Saturday, silly. I brought you another present. Here." Sissy held out a black hat with a wide, floppy brim. A brocade rope was stitched over the seam where the brim met the cap. Squarely in front was a big black flower formed from folded silk ribbon. Two long black sashes hung down for tying under the chin. It was monstrous, like something Bethy's old grandmother would wear to a funeral.

"What am I going to do with a thing like that?" asked Charity.

"You're going to wear it," she said. "I'm going to show you Burlington. Take that silly rag off your head."

Chapter Eight

"No!" said Bea. "Charity's not leaving this room until we're ready to get on the northbound train."

"It's all right, Bea," said Sissy. "She'll be with me."

"What about Hendrick? Did you forget he's out there looking for us?" Bea's eyes were on Charity.

"Bea, he doesn't even know me. He's looking for you," protested Charity. "Besides, I'd rather be dead than stay cooped up in this little room all the time."

"If he finds you, sister, you'll wish you was dead," said Bea. "And I'll wish it for you, too, instead of what he'll put you through."

"No one will ever suspect Charity's a Negro," said Sissy. "She's lighter than Daisy Wires, who's in my class at school. Even if they do, there are Negroes who've been living in Burlington for years, even working here, and nobody has come to take them. Besides, we won't be gone long." Bea slowly turned her back on the girls. Charity had not seen many people talk back to her older sister, and she had never seen her back down in an argument, especially to a girl as flighty as this one. Bea had a way of closing a roof over her thoughts that kept them from escaping or from anyone entering in. Some people were put off by her introversion and thought she was sullen or even rude. Others were intimidated by her quietness, mistaking it for displeasure or anger. A few ignored her completely and went about their own business. Sissy was one of the latter.

She helped Charity remove the cloth that was wrapped around her head. Thick, dark hair fell down in all directions, covering Charity's face and reaching below her shoulders.

"Great gobs of goose grease!" said Sissy. "What a mess. We have to do something about this."

"Help me untangle it," said Charity.

"It would be easier to cut it off," said Sissy, "if I had some scissors."

"Never mind," said Charity. "Do you know how to braid?"

Sissy worked on Charity's hair until she had wound it into a thick pigtail. She tied it with an extra piece of ribbon from her own hair and stood back to inspect her work.

"It will have to do," she said. She adjusted the hat on Charity's head and tied the sash. The ends were so long that even with the generous bow, they still hung almost to her waist. Then she wound a scarf around Charity's neck and pulled it up over her chin. Finally, she pulled the black brim of the bonnet down over one eye. Charity felt like she was looking out from the narrow end of a funnel. But Sissy told her that with her new muslin skirt and wool coat, Charity looked like any other friend of Sissy's who was trying to ward off Vermont's persistent winter weather.

As Charity was about to leave, she felt Bea's hand on her arm. "He's fat, like a Christmas pig. Eyes small as a mole's. Walks with a limp. Hamstring never did heal right after Old

Ben cut it. Took a week for Ben to die after Hendrick got done with him. Watch out for him."

Charity kissed Bea on the cheek and hurried out after Sissy. When she stepped out of the ell, Charity was greeted by gasps of winter winds. The daylight nearly blinded her, and she was glad for the shade of the hat brim. What a different world it was than she had known for the past weeks. The maple trees had outlines, and the ice on the branches flashed silver in the sun. The sky was pale blue with clouds as pink and delicate as the roses in the Primrose flower garden. Even the air smelled different, warmer and safer than in the forbidding darkness. A feeling of ease and contentment settled over Charity, re-placing for a moment the anxiety that had accompanied every action since she left Primrose. Then she shook herself. She couldn't relax and take the feeling of safety for granted. She must remember what Bea had told her.

Charity followed Sissy to the front of the house. Their shad-ows stretched out in front of them as the sun rose up over the hill behind them. A gray field rolled down to a stone quarry carved into the earth, and beyond that was an empty, frozen pasture. Tiny houses dotted the vast field, and horse-drawn carts stood next to some of them. Here and there someone stood by a hole in the ground and held a stick over it. In the distance blue mountains rose up through a haze, and white billows like giant cotton balls swirled down to meet them.

"Why are the houses in the field so small?" asked Charity.

"That's not a field," said Sissy. "It's Lake Champlain. It will be frozen over until April. And those houses are fishing shan-ties. Every one of them sits over a hole in the ice, and men fish through it. You can see some of them fishing out in the open."

The idea of such a vast area of ice was beyond Charity's comprehension. She had read about the Ice Age, but she did not know that it came every winter to the north. She wondered if Canada was like this.

"How do the fish live in the ice?" asked Charity.

Sissy's laughter startled her. "It's only frozen on top. There's water underneath. In the summer when the ice melts, we can swim in it. There are pretty sailboats, and the steamboats come and go all day. It's so big that it takes a steamboat more than an hour to cross over to New York. And those are the Adirondack Mountains." She pointed across the lake. "I've been there with my father when he went to preach a sermon in Plattsburgh. But it's not as nice as here."

Charity was hypnotized by the dramatic beauty of this place. The wind on her cheeks and the smell of morning filled her like a hearty breakfast.

"Good morning, Missy Young." Charity's head involuntarily jerked toward the voice.

"Hello, Mr. Raskin," said Sissy. The postman looked larger up close. He stood next to his horse and lighted a pipe that he held in his teeth. There was a strange glint in his eye. His mailbag was hooked to the saddle of his horse, whose head was bowed toward the ground as if she were willing some grass to pop up through the slushy snow.

"And how are Reverend and Mrs. Young today?"

"They're fine, sir, thank you."

"Who's your little friend?"

"This is . . . Marie. She's visiting this weekend with her family," said Sissy.

"Oh. And where are you from, Marie?"

"She's from Montreal, Mr. Raskin," said Sissy.

"That's a mighty long way to come for a weekend visit," he said. "Can't she speak for herself?"

"She doesn't speak English hardly at all, sir. They speak

French up there. But if you say something in French to her, she might light up."

Jim Raskin raised his eyebrows and puffed on his pipe. "Well, the only French I know is guillotine, but Marie doesn't look like she's encountered one of those," he said, cackling. His horse snorted through her nose as if she were joining in the joke. Charity was amazed at the facility with which Sissy lied. It was hard to believe that this was a minister's daughter.

Mr. Raskin's chuckles faded as a black wagon rattled up the slope of the road. The word "police" was printed on its side. Charity tugged at Sissy's coat in desperation, but Sissy stood firm. Charity pulled the brim of her hat down lower over her eyes, and Sissy squeezed her hand reassuringly.

"Good day, Sam," said Mr. Raskin, touching the top of his hat in salute.

"Morning, Jim," answered the man driving the team of horses. His fat cheeks were red from the cold. A tarnished sheriff's badge was pinned to his coat lapel. Next to him sat a man so thin that his head looked like it had been squeezed in a vise. His eyes were green marbles that barely fit side-by-side on his face. From under a grotesquely large nose, a mass of dark whiskers sprouted. They completely covered his mouth and drooped down past his shaved chin. His whole bearing was ominous. He and the sheriff seemed not to notice the girls.

"This gentleman is looking for a fugitive slave woman, Jim. Goes by the name of Sunday. Rumor has it that she might be at the Bigelow house. She walked in from Tennessee a while back," said the sheriff. Charity looked at Sissy, but she was as still as a mannequin.

"Well." Mr. Raskin dropped the word like an anvil. He walked slowly over and planted his foot on the hub of the

43

sheriff's wagon wheel. "I think you're on the wrong trail, Sam. I just had coffee with Mrs. Bigelow, and there are no black people on the place."

"There's a hundred dollar reward out for her. That would be enough for a man to buy a new horse . . . if he needed one," said the sheriff, and he looked at Jim Raskin's old mare, who shifted her weight from left to right and sighed.

"You don't say," said Mr. Raskin.

"Mr. Sheffield here came all the way from Tennessee, and he'd rather not go home empty-handed," said the sheriff.

Mrs. Bigelow cleared her throat. She stood bundled up on the front porch and glared at the men. She apparently had not seen Charity and Sissy, and they slipped behind a shrub by the side of the house.

The sheriff stared back at Mrs. Bigelow, but he did not acknowledge her. He spoke to Jim Raskin. "If anyone wants more information on her, there's a handbill posted at the Quaker Meeting House with all the details."

"Come to think of it," said Mr. Raskin, "I met a man at the post office this morning. Said he saw a Negro woman heading north on foot about daybreak. Said she looked to him like she might be a fugitive. Said she was aiming toward the woods down to the Intervale."

"Thanks, Jim. If we pick her up, I'm sure you'll get a share of the reward." The sheriff jerked the reins, and the horses stamped forward. The wagon turned up Maple Street and disappeared.

Mrs. Bigelow lifted her skirts slightly as she walked down the porch stairs. "You are a clever man, Jim," she said, "but you may very well have sent them into the path of other fugitives, especially if they bring out the dogs."

"I wouldn't worry too much about that, Mrs. Bigelow," said Mr. Raskin, mounting his horse. "They won't get very far without this." He held up the linchpin to a wheel hub and dropped it into his coat pocket. A crash sounded in the distance, and men's curses sliced the air.

"Still," said Jim Raskin slowly, "a hundred dollars could buy a mighty nice horse." He tipped his hat toward Mrs. Bigelow and rode off.

"Blackmailing devil," said Mrs. Bigelow under her breath, and she marched off toward downtown.

Sissy yanked Charity's hand. "What are you doing?" asked Charity.

"Let's see where she's going," said Sissy. From a safe distance, they followed Mrs. Bigelow along a street of large houses. Charity had never seen such giant structures so close together. They were more narrow than the big house at Primrose, but rose higher into the sky. It hurt her neck to look up at the gables.

Mrs. Bigelow's eyes were fastened forward, and her step was determined. She walked up to the wooden door of a white clapboard house. The sign above the door read "Quaker Meeting." She grabbed the handbill, ripped it into little pieces, and tossed them into the air. The wind lifted and scattered them in all directions.

Chapter Nine

From behind a giant elm tree, Charity and Sissy watched Mrs. Bigelow turn and walk back the way she had come. Then they went west, down Pearl Street.

"Here's our church," said Sissy. "My father's inside right now writing tomorrow's sermon. I wish you could come hear him preach. He's elegant." Charity thought she meant eloquent, but she did not bother to correct her. She had not seen the building in daylight when she and Bea arrived three days before, but it felt familiar, like a remembered dream.

Like many of the buildings in Burlington, the Unitarian Church was red brick. Atop its roof was a wooden spire, painted white, that held a large iron bell. The church sat on a knoll on the north side of Pearl Street, and its front doors looked south, down Church Street, the main thoroughfare in town. Charity could not see Mr. Bigelow's house at the other end of Church Street, beyond the business district, because it was at the bottom of a dip in the road.

Chimes began to sound, the same ones she had heard in the attic. "That's city hall clock," said Sissy. "It should ring ten times if it's right." It was.

"Is Church Street named after your father's church?" asked Charity.

"No, it's named after a lawyer in town. His name is Mr. Church, but I don't think he goes into one very often . . . unless he has a case he's trying to win," Sissy chortled.

Church Street was lined with shops and markets, and several people walked on the wooden boardwalks along the street. The road was rutted with mud, and horses labored in front of full loads. Steam rose from their bodies, and they snorted from the exertion. A few carriages were parked in front of stores, and patient horses pawed the ground and shook their manes while they waited for their drivers. A man was selling popcorn and peanuts from a bright yellow wagon, and Charity could smell the kerosene from the burners mixed with the aroma of the freshly roasted nuts. The lake was on their right. Opposite the lake, the city climbed upward as if trying to get a better view of the New York mountains.

"The University of Vermont is up on the hill," said Sissy. "Girls don't go there, at least not yet. But I'm going to be one of the first graduates. I'm going to study anthropology. That's the study of humans. A man named Charles Darwin says we come from monkeys." Charity had heard about Darwin. Master Pearson said that he should be locked up for heresy. Maybe the Africans were descended from apes, he said, but the white man was created in the image of God. Charity wondered where that left her, with African parents and skin pale as that of many white girls.

"Come on," said Sissy. "Let's go shopping." Charity tried to protest, but Sissy still had her by the hand, so she gave in.

Charity had never been inside a store—she had never had any money to buy anything, anyway—but she had always longed to go when Miss Priscilla took Bethy into Roanoke.

The girls walked south on Church Street, past the jewelers, who also repaired watches, a store that sold music books and instruments, a hardware store, a furniture shop, and businesses that offered shoes, tinware, crockery, glassware, and stoves. Charity paused in front of a window that displayed gallon-sized jars filled with candy in prisms of colors. The letters on the window were stenciled in an arc that spelled out the word "Confectionery." Sissy stopped beside her.

"I have a penny," said Sissy. "Let's go in."

A bell tinkled when they entered, and the smell of peppermint and butterscotch made Charity's mouth water. It was warm inside, and even the air felt sticky-sweet. A counter ran the length of the store. The top half was a glass case that held trays of fudge—white, black, and every shade in between, including tan chunks of peanut butter fudge. Some had pecans and walnuts. There were chocolate-covered cherries and caramels; raisins and hazelnuts were also coated with the sweet, dark stuff.

Behind the counter was a man with a shiny, bald head. His round face supported two chins, and his enormous stomach was covered with a white apron. He glared at the girls when they entered the store.

"No free samples today," he said to Charity. "If you don't have any money, you might as well move on."

"We have money," said Sissy. "We just want to look around first." The fat man frowned at her.

On top of the counter were more glass jars with candies wrapped in paper—silver, gold, red, and green foil. There were lemon drops, jaw breakers, cinnamon drops, malted milk balls, and coconut clusters. Another jar was a vase of lollipops as

48

big as sunflowers, and they looked like pinwheels waiting for a breeze to spin them. From a scale, a tray hung by three thin chains for weighing the nuggets.

"We'll take two of these," said Sissy, pointing to a jar of toffees. Each was wrapped in waxed paper. Charity was disappointed that Sissy had not asked her what she wanted. She would have chosen anything chocolate.

The man took the toffees from the jar and placed them on the counter. Sissy reached up and put her penny next to them. The man said nothing, but turned and punched a button on the cash register. The drawer opened, and he dropped the penny into it.

Outside Charity said, "I never saw such a sour man in such a sweet place." Sissy handed her a toffee. She unwrapped it and popped it into her mouth. It felt like a pencil eraser, but her tongue tasted creamy vanilla. She tried to bite into it, but it was as tough as leather.

"It'll soften up," said Sissy. "Just keep working at it. Best thing about toffee is it lasts a long time." Sissy was right. She was still sucking it out of her teeth when they got to the corner.

"Edward Peck's store is just up Main Street," said Sissy. "I'm supposed to pick up a package there for my father." As they started up the street, a well-dressed man in a top hat strolled toward them. A woman huddled close to him, her gloved hand tucked tightly in the crook of his arm. As they got nearer, Charity could feel the man's eyes on her. She stopped suddenly. Sissy grabbed her coat sleeve and tugged her forward. As they passed, the man reached up and tipped his hat, and the woman smiled and nodded.

"See?" said Sissy. "You're no different from anyone else. Just relax, will you?"

Edward Peck's store was like Aladdin's cave. The walls were

49

lined with merchandise—bolts of bright cloth, shelves of shoes, stacks of blankets and linens. Mittens and hats hung like stalactites from the ceiling. Racks of ready-made clothes held everything from coats to corsets. Glass-front cases glimmered with golden rings and silver watches.

An elderly woman was standing at the counter watching a tall young man cut a piece of red gingham for her. The sleeves of his white shirt were rolled up to his elbows. He chatted happily with the woman, his blue eyes flashing under a tuft of blond hair that fell onto his forehead. He had an angelic face, like pictures on Christmas cards the Pearsons received.

"Don't let his looks fool you," said Sissy. "Willy Peck's as mean as they come. His father owns the store, but if he were for sale, I wouldn't pay two cents for him."

"Thanks for your business, Mrs. Groby," said Willy. "Come back soon." His voice was surprisingly deep, and his white teeth gleamed a broad smile.

"Mind if I just look at the patterns a minute, Will?" she asked.

"Of course not, Mrs. Groby. Help yourself." She walked across the store to a rack that held envelopes of dress patterns. Willy turned toward Sissy and Charity. "Well, if it isn't the elf-child, Miss Sissy Young. What are you doing so far from the North Pole? Santa send you on an errand?"

"I'm just here to pick up something for my father, Willy. Could I have it, please, and then we'll be going."

"We? Is this another one of Santa's helpers?"

"This is Marie. She's a friend of mine."

"How come I've never seen you around, Marie? Or have I? Take off that fine bonnet and let's have a look at you."

"Marie's shy, Willy. She's from Montreal. She doesn't know anyone in Burlington besides me. Now, where's that package?"

"You may have gotten that hat in Montreal, but your coat looks like it came from Edward Peck's store. The skirt, too. But I'm sure I've never seen you in here before, Marie."

"Willy, this is my coat, if it's any of your business," said Sissy, pointing at Charity's jacket. "And it's my skirt, too. We traded clothes. Don't you know anything about women?"

"I've never seen you wearing that coat. Looks to me like all you ever wear is this old rag you've had on all winter." Mrs. Groby turned and peered at the trio. Willy cleared his throat. "Of course, it looks fine on you, Sissy," he said and grinned at Mrs. Groby.

"Marie gave me her petticoat to wear. And if you ask me to show it to you, I'll tell your father you've been fresh."

"Ahem," said Mrs. Groby. "I'll be going now, Will. Say hello to your father for me."

"Yes, ma'am. Good day, Mrs. Groby," said Willy. When Mrs. Groby had gone, Willy looked at Charity. "What's wrong with you, Marie? Cat got your tongue? Or are you just simple? You'd have to be to hang around with a little trollop like Sissy here."

"Leave her alone, Willy. I told you, she's from Montreal. They speak French up there. She probably thinks you're an idiot." Willy ignored Sissy. His eyes were still on Charity.

"You ever see any runaway slaves up in Montreal, Marie? I hear the town's full of them, living like they were free people. I'd sure like to get my hands on one of 'em. I'd sell him in a heartbeat to one of those slave traders, like that fat man who's been hanging around the store lately."

"What man?" asked Sissy.

"Calls himself Henry or Henderson or something like that. He walks with a cane. Has a bad limp." Charity looked at Sissy.

51

"We have to be going, Willy. I'll get that package later," said Sissy, turning to leave.

"Wait a minute," said Willy. "Here's a little souvenir for Marie. That's a French word, isn't it, Marie?" Willy reached for a tray of hatpins on the counter and selected one that had a brass ball on the end. "Courtesy of Peck's store."

"Willy," said Sissy, "what would your father say if he knew you were giving away merchandise?"

"I'd run him out of business if I could. He cares more about sneaking those stinking fugitives north than he cares about what I'm doing." Willy lifted the brim of Charity's bonnet and pinned it back against the cap. "Say, you're a pretty little thing," he said. Charity looked up through her dark lashes. Without the shadow of the hat brim, she felt exposed.

Sissy shoved Charity toward the door. "Good-bye, Willy Peck," she called without looking back.

"Hey, Sissy," called Willy after them. "If your daddy gets in another load of black baggage, you let me know, hear? Maybe I'll buy one off him cheap and make a little profit from Mr. Henderson."

When they were a safe distance from the store, Charity said, "That's the man who's looking for Bea and me."

"Maybe not," said Sissy. "It could just be a coincidence. And Willy has a bad habit of making things up."

"But how would he know about the limp? I've got to get back to Bea."

"Okay, okay. But come down to the lake with me for a minute first. I just have one more thing to show you."

Chapter Ten

The train station at the bottom of College Street was a long, gray building two stories high. Below a Western Union sign was a notice of the arrival and departure times for the trains. The next one left for Montreal at 10:28. It must be close to that now, Charity thought.

People walked about in front of the station, some hurrying with suitcases or bundles, others sauntering. A few men stood outside, leaning on wagons and watching people come and go.

"Slave hunters," Sissy said. They were lean and hungry looking. Charity felt a hot tingle on her neck in spite of the chilly air. "Almost as low as slave traders. The law ought to be against them instead of you."

Behind the station the train was warming up to leave. Charity had never been so close to a locomotive. She could have stood within the circumference of a wheel. It was a gigantic iron dinosaur with steam spouting from its open neck. A huge piston pumped up and down on its back. Attached to its front was a wide plow, which Sissy said was called a cow-catcher. Charity felt sorry for the cows or anything else that got in its way. Behind it was the tender, which carried the wood for the engine, and following it were a dozen passenger cars, most of them dark green trimmed with gold.

The train was heading north. This might be the very train she and Bea would ride in a few days, Charity thought. And when it started to move, with its size and power, no slave hunter, however determined, could turn it around and take them back.

The conductor leaned out the door of a car and waved at the engineer. Sissy was saying something about the station when the train whistle blew. It was so loud that Charity could only see Sissy's mouth moving.

The train began to inch forward, like a giant caterpillar, slowly picking up speed. After the last car left the station, Charity watched it disappear down the tracks, feeling sorry to see it leave without her. Soon, Bea had said, soon it would be their turn, and she would watch out the window as the land of slavery slipped away behind her.

When the train was gone, Charity had a clear view of the frozen lake. Sissy crossed the railroad tracks, and Charity was close behind her. They made their way toward one of the two piers that jutted out from shore. A few people leaned on the railing. Charity walked down the slope beside the pier and stopped at the edge of the ice.

The fishing shanties looked larger close up. "Why don't the horses and the wagons fall in?" said Charity. "They look awfully heavy."

"The ice is about a foot thick," said Sissy. "Go on and walk on it." Charity took a tentative step onto the ice. With her second step both feet flew out from under her and she landed hard on her bottom. Sissy laughed. "Slide your feet; don't pick them up. Like this," she said, and she slid around in circles on the hard surface. Charity joined her, cautiously at first. Then she, too, was sliding, and, although she fell a few more times, she slid and turned until she was panting. She glided toward Sissy, arms out, and they grabbed each other and rotated in a tight circle until they were both dizzy. They fell onto the ice, arms and legs tangled, out of breath.

"Whoo-ee!" said Charity. "If Bethy could see this, she'd find a way to get Master Pearson to buy her one."

"A skating pond? Good luck, Bethy. A couple days of her warm southern winters and she'd go right through. It takes months of freezing to get like this. But a warm spell will melt it right down."

"Look over there," said Charity. They were out beyond the end of the pier. Just to the north some children and a few adults were gliding across the lake on skates, their silver blades sparkling. They were hardly moving their legs, except for the children who appeared to be just learning to skate. They were little bundled beetles, scurrying to keep their balance and often falling on their backs, waving arms and legs in the air. Some older boys had long sticks and were hitting a ball to one another. They were trying to get it past another boy, who was protecting a goal made with two piles of coats. Even in the cold wind they had worked up a sweat. By now fishermen grouped in twos or threes huddled over their fishing holes, and the whole scene was like a winter circus.

"Let's go out to the breakwater," said Sissy, and she headed farther out onto the ice without waiting for a response. Charity slipped along behind her. The breakwater was a long, low stone wall with small lighthouses at each end. It ran along the shore about a quarter of a mile out. Charity guessed that it kept the water calm in the harbor when there was no ice. The few people out this far were off to either side a good way. The ice had cracks in it here and there. One long crack was almost an inch wide, and Charity could see that the ice was thick. She wanted to call to her new friend to come back, but she would not allow Sissy to think she was afraid. Besides, Charity thought, Sissy probably ventured out this far all the time.

Charity carefully stepped over the crack, and as she did, she saw something move beneath her feet. She lost her balance and dropped to her knees, grabbing at the flat ice to steady herself. It stung her bare hands, but the ice was perfectly still. It had not moved. Then she saw it again, a metallic glint of light under the surface. She followed it with her eyes until she saw several more, like knives flashing in the sun.

"Fish," said Sissy. She had come back to see what Charity was doing on all fours. "This is black ice. You can see right through it. It's the closest I've ever come to walking on water."

Charity had seen the men pulling small fish up through the holes in the ice, but it seemed an isolated act, separate from the activity that went on below. The frozen layer was like armor that, at least for a few months of the year, protected the life underneath from the swirling currents created by the paddleboats and steamships, and the intrusions of fishing lines and kicking legs. It seemed unjust, then, that these persistent anglers invaded the private territory beneath winter's shield to snag an unsuspecting creature.

"Well, there it is," said Sissy, breaking into Charity's thoughts. "I said I'd show you Burlington. Have a look."

Charity stood up. She felt like she was on the stage of an amphitheater, and the city provided the seats rising up to the bases of Vermont's two largest mountains. Perhaps the whole town was in attendance, watching her perform her act, a fugitive slave having a holiday with a Yankee white girl.

Burlington was a patchwork of small, urban farms, stitched together with split rail fences. The domed mansion of the university dominated the landscape. Greek revival government buildings and large Federal homes occupied the downtown area. Sprinkled in between were small wood frame houses where common folks lived. Factories and lumberyards were closest to the lake. It was the lake that gave the town its purpose. Even in its dormant state, Charity could feel its vitality.

To the south was the second pier, and beyond that men were out on the ice with saws. They were working feverishly to break the ice into large blocks, which they loaded onto low sleds drawn by horses.

"What in heaven's name are they doing?" asked Charity.

"They're cutting ice. What does it look like?" said Sissy. "It gets stored in the stone house there on the shore, and it stays frozen all summer long."

"I don't believe this place ever gets hot enough to thaw ice." Charity blew on her hands to warm them.

"Oh, this is just the beginning of mud season," said Sissy. "But the sap is starting to run. You'll see buckets hanging on the sugar maples. The sap dripping into them makes a happy song. After sugaring season, it gets hot all of a sudden, even before school's out. Pretty soon the steamboats will be running again, taking maple sugar and lumber north to Canada. We can come down and watch them. They sure are a sight."

"I won't be here long enough to see the ice melt," Charity reminded her. "I'll be in Canada before your maple sugar will."

"Oh . . . right," said Sissy, looking across the ice at the snow-covered Adirondacks. Clouds were starting to move in, and the ice field turned pale gray. "Let's go into the Lake House and warm up."

Charity followed Sissy back toward the railroad station. Next door was a small hotel where a red omnibus drawn by four horses waited by the entrance. The girls went into the lobby and stamped their feet and rubbed their hands together. Charity pulled the scratchy scarf from her chin and let the warm air reach her neck. She was about to tell Sissy she had better get back to Bea when a tall, handsome man came in through the front door. His skin was as dark as Bea's. He was dressed in a black suit and a starched white shirt with a neatly tied bow at his neck, and he wore a trim felt hat. He looked like he was going to a formal ball. When he saw the girls, he reached up and took off his hat.

"Hello, Nate," said Sissy.

"Good afternoon, Miss Cecilia," he said.

"Are you on your way to work?" she asked.

"I sure am. But I have a minute to ask you how your folks are doing."

"They're just fine, Nate. And this is my friend, Charity."

"How do you do, Miss Charity," said Nate.

Charity was not sure whether she should hide behind her hat brim and scarf or whether it was safe to be herself. Who was this black man who walked proudly past slave catchers as if there were no price on his head? She let Sissy take the lead.

"And how are Tess and Lida?" asked Sissy.

"Couldn't be better."

"Tell them hey for me, will you, Nate?"

"I have a better idea, Miss Cecilia. Why don't you stop in and tell them hey yourself? Tess was making some oatmeal cookies when I left, and they're probably still warm. And I'm sure Lida would like to see you, and your friend Charity, too. Gotta get to work now. Lunch time gets pretty busy. Y'all have a good day. Good seeing you, Miss Cecilia. You, too, Miss Charity." He turned and walked into the dining room of the hotel.

"Who was that?" asked Charity.

"Oh, just a friend of mine," said Sissy, casually.

"But why don't the slave catchers take him away?"

"Nate's been in Burlington as long as I can remember. He has a job and a family, and everybody in town knows him. He's as free as I am. Besides," Sissy added, "anybody who bothers Nate has to answer to Mr. Bigelow."

Charity would have liked to believe it was possible to live in the states without hiding. But somehow it seemed like a false hope. She rubbed her eyes. Pungent cigar smoke was making them tear. She looked around the lobby. On a leather sofa sat a man, fat as a Christmas pig, puffing on the butt of a cigar. His molelike eyes were studying the *Burlington Daily News*. A cane leaned against his knee. Sissy saw him, too.

"Act natural," she said. "Walk slowly. I'm right behind you."

Chapter Eleven

"That was him. Did he see me?" said Charity. They were on the sidewalk outside the hotel.

"He never looked up," said Sissy. "That bonnet works like a charm."

Charity reached up to adjust the brim of the bonnet and put her hand on the hatpin Willy had given her. "I'd better let this down," she said. She fumbled with the pin, and the point stuck her finger. It pricked the skin deeply, and blood oozed from the puncture. "Ow!" said Charity.

"You'd better suck it," said Sissy. "Here. Let me get that for you."

Charity stuck her finger into her mouth while Sissy removed the pin. The brim flopped down in front of Charity's face.

"Think your friend Willy planned that to happen?"

"I wouldn't put it past him. 'Course, maybe you just don't know your way around hatpins." Sissy wove the pin into the lapel of Charity's coat. "There. Next time grab it by the dull end."

Of course she knew how to handle a hatpin, Charity thought. She helped Bethy with one nearly every day.

"I'd better get back to Mr. Bigelow's house," said Charity. "I'll have to warn Bea."

"Nate's house is on the way," said Sissy. "Tess'll have a bandage for your finger."

Charity pulled the scarf back over her chin. The girls walked up College Street to Pine and turned south. Sissy stopped at a white clapboard house with green shutters and hammered the brass knocker. A pretty young woman opened the door. She was carrying a baby who had three stubby little fingers stuck in her mouth.

"Why, Cecilia Young. Lida and I were just talking about you, weren't we, honey?" she said, and smiled at Lida, who did not answer. "You come right on in and have a visit with us. Lida's been a handful today, and she could use a distraction."

Lida pointed a finger at Sissy. A string of drool followed it from her mouth. "Sis-sis," she said.

"Hey, Lida," said Sissy, and she pinched Lida's nose gently. "Tess, this is my friend, Charity."

"Pleased to meet you, Charity. You're welcome, too," she said.

"Hello," said Charity.

Inside Tess took their coats and hung them on pegs in the entryway. Charity grabbed the bow under her chin that held her hat on and looked at Sissy with an expression that verged on panic.

"Take your hat off, Charity," said Sissy. "You don't need it in here." Charity untied the sash and handed the hat to Tess.

"That sure is a nice hat," said Tess. "I don't blame you for wanting to leave it on." She hung the hat on a peg with Charity's coat.

They walked through a tiny living room. Except for a few of Lida's toys, it was tidy. The furniture was not the fine quality that was in the big house at Primrose, but it was well cared for and looked comfortable. A small stove in a corner warmed the room.

The girls followed Tess and Lida into the kitchen, and Tess put Lida down. She stood a minute, clinging to her mother's skirt, then toddled over to Sissy. Sissy sat on a chair at the kitchen table, picked Lida up, and sat her on her lap. She rubbed the woolly curls on the baby's head, and Lida tried to put her wet fingers into Sissy's mouth.

"Yucky," said Sissy. Lida giggled.

"Have you had lunch? I've got a pot of hot corn chowder here," said Tess. She ladled some out into two bowls and placed one in front of each girl. She gave Lida a cookie to keep her busy while the girls ate. All her movements were small and quiet, as if she did not want to call attention to herself. Each action was exact and efficient. Even her body had no waste. She was barely taller than Charity and couldn't have weighed much more. Her hair was brushed back and pinned against her head. Her face was as carefully sculpted as cut crystal.

"What were you saying about me?" asked Sissy with her mouth half full.

"When?" said Tess.

"Before we came. You said you and Lida were talking about me," said Sissy.

"Oh, yes. Well, Mr. Bigelow stopped by on his way to work at the newspaper yesterday morning."

"What for?" said Sissy.

"Just let me get one question answered before you start another one, young lady," said Tess, laughing. She laughed easily.

"Sorry," said Sissy.

"He stops by occasionally to see how we are," Tess said slowly, as if explaining to Lida. "Anyway," she continued, "he said that two young women are staying in the ell and that you have become friends with them."

"Yes, she has," said Charity.

"Well, would one of them happen to be named Charity?" she asked, and she worked up a playful frown. Charity and Sissy's silence was an affirmation.

Charity's finger had stopped bleeding, but it still hurt, and she held her soup spoon awkwardly. When she dropped it into the chowder, it clattered against the bowl.

"Something wrong with your hand?" asked Tess.

"I'll say. She stuck Willy Peck's hatpin into it. You have anything to put on it?" said Sissy.

"What are you doing with Willy's hatpin, Charity?"

"He . . . he gave it to me. I guess it was a present."

"Willy took a fancy to Charity," said Sissy.

"But Willy Peck hates black people. He tells me, 'Why don't you go on back to Africa.' Isn't that just ignorant? How can I go back to where I've never been? He won't wait on me when I go into the store, either. I have to call for Mr. Peck. He sure is a nice man. I can't understand how he raised a bigot for a son."

"Willy thinks she's white," said Sissy. "We told him her name is Marie and she's from Montreal."

"And he believed you?" Tess threw her head back and laughed at the ceiling. "Lord, have mercy! Well, I'm not about to tell your secret," she said. She pointed a finger at Charity. "But you just be careful around that boy. He'd sell his mama if he thought she had a drop of African blood." She went to the cupboard and pulled out a piece of cotton and some tape and began to wrap it around Charity's finger.

"Yum, yum, yum-m-m," said Lida. She was scooping Sissy's soup out of the bowl and ladling it into her mouth with the hand that was not holding the cookie. Tess concentrated on Charity's puncture.

"Where are you from, Charity?"

Charity hesitated. She knew that some slaves had been forced into betraying others, but Tess's ingenuousness made her feel that secrets would be safe here. "Virginia, ma'am," she said finally.

"Now don't go ma'aming me. I'm not much older than you. You call me Tess."

"Yes . . . Tess," said Charity.

"I've never been to Virginia," said Tess. "Tell me what it's like."

"In the summer it gets so hot you can hardly stand it unless you stay in the shade," said Charity. "It gets so hazy, the mountains look blue, and it always smells like honeysuckle. The winter never gets as cold as here. It snows every now and then, but it never stays long." Charity was itching with questions for Tess, too. How could she live on her own without answering to a white master when she and Bea were sneaking and hiding to get to freedom? "How long have you been here, Tess?"

"Twenty years come my birthday this May," Tess said. "I was born here in Burlington. My folks live in Winooski. That's the next town over. In fact, I've never been out of Vermont, not counting once when Nate and I rode the steamboat to New York and back."

"But who do you answer to?" asked Charity.

"I don't answer to anyone, Charity, unless you count Nate.

64

A lot of Negroes in the north were born free. My parents were slaves on a farm in Pennsylvania. When the farmer died, his wife gave them their freedom, and they came farther north to start their lives over. I hope by the time Lida is grown, slavery will be something you read about in history books." Lida turned her attention to the cookie, which was now soggy, and squished it between her fingers. Tess went to the stove where water was boiling in the kettle and prepared a pot of tea.

"What about Nate?" asked Charity.

Sissy broke in. "Lida, you are the messiest little girl I've ever seen," she said. Lida had smeared the cookie on the backs of Sissy's hands, and some soup had dripped onto the sleeves of her dress. Tess handed her a damp cloth. A skinny tabby cat strolled into the kitchen. It rubbed languorously against Tess' skirt and meowed.

"Ditty!" Lida squealed. She scooted off Sissy's lap and toddled after the cat.

"What about Nate?" Charity said again. She wanted to know. "Is he free, too?"

Tess brought the pot of tea to the table. She picked up the empty soup bowls and carried them to the sink. She brought back three cups and a plate of cookies, and placed them on the table. All this was done in silence. Charity searched Tess's face. The easy smile was gone. She pulled out a third chair and softly sat down. Lida was playing with the cat.

"Yes, he is free, Charity," said Tess at last. "He ran to freedom just like you. He came to Vermont almost three years ago. He wanted to stay here rather than go to Canada. Mr. Bigelow got him a job as a waiter in the restaurant at the Lake House, and he helped us buy our home." She poured three cups of tea before she spoke again. "I just hope this story has a happily-ever-after ending."

"Of course it will," said Sissy. "No one has bothered you all this time."

Lida screeched. "Hur' me ditty," she said, tears filling her big brown eyes. She was holding up a hand for her mother to see.

"Oh, dear," said Tess, and she went to pick up the baby.

"I've got to get back to my sister," said Charity. "I hope I see you again, Tess, before . . ." She had learned not to anticipate farther than the present. The sentence dangled in the air for a moment. Then Tess made Sissy promise to bring Charity back if she could. She hugged Charity tightly with her right arm, holding Lida in her left. "Good luck, Charity," she said. "God be with you."

Chapter Twelve

Sissy walked Charity back to the ell, and they slipped unnoticed through the back door. Charity removed the bonnet and pushed it toward her friend. Sissy took it and wrapped her arm around Charity's neck. When she kissed Charity firmly on the cheek, the smell of lavender flashed images of spring flowers through Charity's mind. Sissy promised to come back the next day and then disappeared back into the cold afternoon. Charity ran up the steps, two at a time, and paused, out of breath, in front of the door to the attic. No sound came from the other side. She pushed the door open. For a moment she was blinded by fear, and then she focused on the empty room. Bea and Sunday were gone. Her eyes searched from wall to wall, from floor to apex, to be sure Bea was not just hiding from her, as Bethy sometimes did. But Bea was not one to play jokes. Nothing was disturbed. There was no sign of struggle. The silence of the still room enveloped her like a cold night, and she felt suddenly alone. She hugged herself and shivered. Bea wasn't well enough to travel, and Charity knew she wouldn't have left her behind. She thought of Hendrick, his fierce little eyes crowded by his meaty jowls. He could not have found Bea that quickly. In fact, he didn't seem in any hurry at all. Maybe Mr. Bigelow had moved her, and Sunday, too, but where? Then she remembered Isaac and George in the cellar, and she clambered down the stairs.

In the alcove she knocked on the wall panel. "It's Charity," she yelled, and now she didn't care who heard her. The panel slid aside, and Isaac stood before her. He was not smiling this time. "Bea's gone," said Charity desperately.

"Be quiet, child," said Isaac. "Your sister is here."

Charity pushed past him and stumbled into the cellar room. Sunday was sitting on the ledge by the tunnel with George. On the far side of the room a man lay on a cot. A cloth rested on his forehead, and his shoulder was bandaged. Bea sat beside him on a low stool. Charity walked to her sister and knelt next to her. She put her head on Bea's lap, and Bea stroked her hair softly. After a minute Charity looked at the wounded man and asked, "What happened?"

It was Isaac who answered. "Mr. Bigelow brought him in early this morning." He nodded toward the cot. "Mr. Young helped carry him, and Mr. Wires, too. He's traveled a good ways, looks like, and had a rough time of it. Someone wants him back pretty bad. Bad enough to slow him down by putting some shot in him."

"It's just a flesh wound," said Bea. "But he's lost some blood, and he's real weak. We'll need to watch for infection."

"The doctor was not able to come," said Isaac. "Mr. Bigelow said men have been watching the house, and it's too dangerous. Your sister is a fine nurse, though. He'll be up and about in no time. Meanwhile, you had better make yourself comfortable in your new quarters." Charity looked at him quizzically.

"We best move down here," said Sunday. "If they search Mr. Bigelow's house, they're likely to start with the attic. I doubt they'll find their way to the cellar, but if they do, we can leave through the tunnel." Charity remembered Sissy's books, but Sunday anticipated her thoughts. "Mrs. Bigelow will bring your books and things down tonight." Charity sat back on her heels and breathed a sigh.

For the first time she became aware of an odor in the room. It seemed to emanate from the cot where the strange man lay. It was like the smell in the kitchen at Primrose when Penny had caught a rat in a trap she had set in one of the cupboards. The rat had apparently been dead for days before she discovered it, and they dug a hole and buried it beyond the garden. It was many more days before the smell completely left the kitchen. Charity wondered whether the man on the cot was dying, or perhaps he was already dead. His brown eyelids were drawn over bulging eyeballs. The short, black lashes were tightly curled. His nose was nearly flat against his face. His jaw was relaxed, and his mouth hung open. A pink tongue undulated behind ivory teeth as he breathed in and out. His chest rose and fell almost imperceptibly with each breath. He was alive, all right. But barely.

"Is there anything I can do?" asked Charity to no one in particular.

"I was just reading to George. All I could find was this book of poetry," said Isaac, handing it to Charity. "I'm afraid there's not much to suit a boy. But perhaps you'd read us all a little."

Charity took off her coat and dropped it onto an empty bed. She sat next to George and thumbed through the book. The pages fell open to a section of poems by Alfred, Lord Tennyson. She read poems about the noble death of King

Arthur and of Ulysses, the hero of the Trojan War, who struggled to return to his family. When she finished, the cellar settled into quiet. After a few minutes Sunday softly began to hum an old hymn, and Isaac added a baritone harmony. George fell asleep with his head on Charity's shoulder. There was so much that she wanted to tell Bea, but it would have to wait.

Chapter Thirteen

By evening it was obvious that Bea was feeling better. Sunday made some food in the makeshift kitchen and gave each of them a plate. Bea took hers and sat on the empty cot, pushing Charity's coat aside. She pulled her feet up and covered them with her skirt, sitting cross-legged while she ate. Bea looked at the coat again and paused with the spoon halfway between plate and mouth. She put the spoon down and pulled the coat closer to examine the hatpin.

"What's this?" Bea asked.

"It's a . . . you know . . . a hatpin."

"Where'd it come from?"

No answer.

"I asked you a question, girl."

"Sissy gave it to me." She had never lied to Bea before, but how could she tell her a white boy had given it to her because he thought she was pretty?

"You sure you didn't steal it? Don't need no more trouble than we got."

"No, Bea, I didn't steal it."

"What's it doing on your coat? Where's that big old hat you was wearing?"

"I gave it back. I won't need it anymore. We're almost to Canada now. Are you well enough to move on?"

"We need to take a little more time," said Bea. She turned to look at the wounded man. "He needs to be watched. You got to be patient, sister."

"But Bea," said Charity, "I saw Hendrick."

"Where?"

"At the hotel near the railroad station."

Bea pushed the food around on her plate with her spoon.

"Bea? Did you hear me? We've got to go. There are others, too. Slave catchers everywhere."

"I hear you. We came this far, didn't we? We'll go when the time's right. Now hush," Bea said, putting an end to the discussion.

Charity couldn't figure Bea out. Before, she couldn't be persuaded to stop for more than a night anywhere. Something was making Charity feel uneasy in this cellar. She realized she felt more safe outside posing as a white girl than she did hiding as a slave. As Sissy's friend, people ignored her or smiled kindly. But here she was a fugitive, and danger seemed to surround her.

She was restless. She wanted to be on the road again, moving away from Hendrick and Sheffield and Willy Peck. She wanted a home where she could be herself and not sneak around like a hunted animal.

Charity finished eating and turned her attention to George, who was now playing with some pebbles on the floor. He had formed two lines of them, and one by one he was moving them toward each other.

"Who are the two teams?" asked Charity.

"They're not teams," said George. "They're soldiers. This is us Northerners fighting against the Southerners, and we're beatin' 'em."

"What's your strategy?" said Charity.

"Huh?" said George.

"How are the Northerners beating the Southerners?"

"We got bigger guns," said George.

"But you're from the south, George," said Charity.

"Not anymore. I'm a Yankee now."

"Me, too, George," said Charity. There had been talk of war at almost every stop on their journey, especially in the north. The Southerners had more to lose by going to war, but the issue of slavery was not going to go away. She also knew that keeping black people ignorant was a stronger weapon than any of the white man's guns.

Charity got an idea. "Hey, George, how would you like to learn how to read?"

"Yeah. I been meaning to learn me how to read."

Charity liked Bethy's tutor and often thought she might want to be a teacher someday. This was her chance to practice. Mrs. Bigelow had brought down the books with her other things. Charity picked out *Last of the Mohicans* and sat down with George. First she showed him the letters of the alphabet and told him what sound they made. Then she showed him some simple words. George was a fast learner, and Charity was a natural at teaching. When she finished with George, she would teach Bea.

A moan from the wounded man's bed distracted them. He was beginning to wake up. Bea went to him and wiped his brow with a cloth. He opened his eyes and looked at her. Isaac was standing behind Bea, and when the man saw him, he jerked away from them, hitting his good shoulder against the wall. He winced, quickly burying the expression as if willing

73

the pain away. He said nothing, but his eyes darted around the room.

"It's all right, man," said Isaac. "We're friends." This information did not appear to comfort him. He tried to get up, nearly knocking Bea off her stool.

"Whoa, there," said Isaac. "You're wounded. You've lost some blood. Better take it easy for a while."

"Who you workin' for?" he said, almost spitting out the words.

"None of us works for anyone except ourselves," said Isaac. "We're all fugitives, just like you, on our way north. This is a hiding place. A man named Bigelow and two others brought you here last night. They're good men. You were in pretty bad shape. Looks like you met up with a bullet."

"White man?" he asked.

"Yes," said Isaac.

"Huh," he laughed sardonically. "Don't trust no white man. I'll be leavin' tonight." He tried to stand, bracing himself against the wall with his good arm. He was naked to the waist, and his chest and arms looked as hard as iron. When he stood, his head nearly reached the beams that supported the main floor of the house. He most likely could crush a man with his bare hands, Charity thought, and, from the look in his eye, he probably would if provoked.

"You're not going anywhere until your shoulder's better. Sit back down now." It was Bea who spoke the command. "Shape you're in, you'll end up right back where you came from—if you don't die first." Charity thought she saw a look of surprise cross his face. He fell back onto the cot. He took his time looking Bea over, and her eyes looked right back at him.

"Who you," he said. It was a command rather than a question.

"Name's Bea."

"You do this?" he said, moving his head toward his bandaged shoulder. Bea barely nodded. He continued to look at her, and Bea returned his stare. Charity sensed a tension in the silent room that she couldn't identify. This man projected a power she had never felt from a black man before. He seemed to have no fear, and Charity thought he would indeed have left the cellar if Bea had not stopped him.

"I'm George. You been out cold all day." Charity had forgotten about George sitting beside her. He put the book down and went over to examine the man more closely. "Why you smell so bad?"

"What are you saying, boy?" said the man.

"You smell like you been rolling in dead animals," said George.

It was true, he did, but Charity wasn't sure if it was a good idea to bring it up until they determined more about this man's mood.

"That's a good smell," he said. "Saved my life more than once. I made this perfume out of scat and the entrails of animals I snared. Rubbed it all over me. Covers up my scent so the bloodhounds get all confused. Pretty soon they just give up. You want me to rub some on you, so you don't smell it so good?"

"No," George said emphatically.

"Maybe you'd like a bath," said Sunday. "I'll heat up some water and fill up the washtub." The man was still concerned with George.

"You got a name?" asked George.

"Franklin. Franklin Boggs. You running away, too?"

"Yeah."

"This your mother?" asked Franklin, motioning toward Bea with his head.

"No. Ain't got a mother. How'd you get here?"

75

"Maybe Mr. Boggs ought to try and eat something before he goes off answering all your questions," said Sunday. "You a little hungry, Franklin?"

"I could eat. Ain't had much but roots and tubers—and grubs when I could find 'em. Snared some animals, when I got lucky." Sunday brought him a bowl of stew and some bread, and he ate like a half-starved animal, holding the bowl up to his mouth with the hand of his wounded side and scooping it in with his good one. When he was finished, Bea took the bowl back to the kitchen and brought him water.

"Drink," she said. "Got to build your blood back up."

Franklin stared at her for a minute. Charity had seen that look only once before, and that was from her father. His eyes bored into her as if trying to find an answer to an unasked question. Like her father, this was a man to be cautious around. He took the mug from Bea's hands and drank, his eyes never leaving hers.

"Water's ready," said Sunday. "The man's going to need some help with this tub. Isaac, can you give me a hand?" Isaac helped Franklin to the kitchen, and Sunday began to strip off what remained of his clothes. "I've seen plenty of bare bottoms in my day, so don't go getting shy on me now," she said. Franklin was surprisingly passive and showed no signs of modesty. He looked over his shoulder from time to time to see if Bea was watching, but she was busy straightening the covers of his bed. Isaac helped him into the washtub. Franklin had his back to the main part of the room, and Charity saw that it was striped with scars. Thick welts like a nest of garter snakes crisscrossed his skin. She felt sick and had to look away.

When his bath was finished, Sunday helped Franklin put on some new clothes that Mr. Bigelow had sent over from Edward Peck's. Isaac helped him back to the cot, and he sat on it sideways, leaning his back against the wall.

"Now will you tell me how you got here?" asked George.

"The man has to rest," said Bea.

"I'll tell the boy some stories," said Franklin. Bea's expression showed that she did not like being overruled. "I came all the way from New Orleans. My mama was an African and my daddy was a Seminole Indian. I don't remember him much. I went with my mama when she was sold for slave work, and we never saw him again." He put a bare foot up on the bed and rested his good arm on it. His hand hung poised in the air like a giant paw. George was sitting on a stool soaking up Franklin's story. "When I was as old as you I was sold to another plantation. Worked in salt boggs, picking cotton, building barns, and any hard labor the man could find for me to do. I ran away from all of them. Got caught every time except the last one."

"They beat you for running off?" asked George.

"Yea. Probably would have killed me, 'cept I guess they figured I was worth more on the auction block than I was dead. But wasn't many who'd bid on me 'cause I look them in the eye instead of hanging my head. You remember that—always look 'em in the eye so they don't think they better than you." He lifted the mug and took a drink. Then he placed the mug on the floor and lay down on the cot with his head on a pillow. He yawned and rubbed his eyes with one hand. When he spoke again, his voice was slow and heavy.

"Last few months I been living in caves and swamps and anywhere I could get out of the way of the hounds." The pauses stretched out between the words. Soon they stopped completely, and Franklin was asleep.

Charity felt like a dangerous animal had been locked back in its cage. She looked around for a safe place to hide the next time the cage door opened.

Chapter Fourteen

That night, Charity dreamed of serpentine monsters chasing her through a viney jungle. They tangled in her hair and wrapped around her legs. The grass was like knife blades slashing at her ankles. She awoke in a sweat and heard the city hall clock chime six times.

Bea got up and began to stir around in the kitchen. Charity pulled herself out of bed, went to the table, and lit a candle to read by. In the flickering light, she could see that Sunday's cot was empty.

"Where's Sunday?" Charity asked Bea.

"She's gone," said Bea.

"Gone where?" asked Charity.

"North," said Bea.

Charity had not imagined the cellar without Sunday. And she had not had a chance to say good-bye or to make plans to meet again on the other side of the border.

"But how—when?" she asked.

Isaac was up by this time, and he gave Charity the details

of Sunday's escape. "Mr. Bigelow came down in the middle of the night. He said a man from Tennessee was getting too persistent with his questions about her. He's been hanging around Mr. Bigelow's newspaper office and bothering Mrs. Bigelow at home. He threatened to call in a federal marshal to search the house. Mr. Bigelow said he'd like to see that federal marshal; he had a complaint to file about invasion of privacy. He thought it best to get Sunday out of town." He poured himself a cup of steaming coffee. "Reverend Young was on the other side of the tunnel waiting for her to crawl through, and Mr. Wires was waiting behind the seminary with a wagon. They drove her up to St. Albans. She'll be on the first train leaving for Montreal this morning. Should be there by noon. But I think Reverend Young may be a little groggy when he preaches his sermon today."

Today was Sunday. At Primrose she would be going to services with her family. They were all like brothers and sisters on the plantation, and their closeness filled the emptiness Charity felt when her mother left. Now there was a new void with Sunday's leaving. At least she still had Bea. And there was little George. But he and Isaac and Franklin, too, would go when their time came. And she could not count on seeing Sissy again. A fugitive had to learn not to leave her heart out in the open where pieces could be cut out. It should be locked in a box and buried deep inside. Only when she was free would she dare to unlock the box again.

Charity read a little more, and Bea went to check on Franklin. He was sitting up, and Charity could feel his eyes on her. "Who's the little white woman with the books?" he asked Bea.

"That's my sister. Name's Charity."

"Half sister, look to me like," he said. "Not much African about her." Charity looked at him for an explanation. Bea

79

said nothing, but Charity sensed her agitation. "Guess I know who her father is." Bea was still silent.

"How do you know my father?" demanded Charity. She could not remember ever seeing Franklin at Primrose, or anywhere else for that matter.

"I don't," Franklin said. "Already know more slave owners than I care to." Charity felt confused. Her father was a slave; he didn't own slaves. Franklin must be delirious from his wound. Otherwise, what was this man saying?

"Bea . . . " said Charity. Bea was glaring at Franklin. She crossed the room to Charity and put a hand on her hair.

"Just read your books," she said. But Charity had trouble concentrating.

The room grew lighter, and Charity knew the sun was rising. This morning the cellar had a gloomy feeling, and she wished George would wake up and add some life to the atmosphere. Presently the secret panel slid open, and Mr. Bigelow entered the room.

"Good morning," he said pleasantly.

"Morning, sir," said Isaac.

"Good morning, Mr. Bigelow," said Charity. Bea nodded. Franklin said nothing. George sat up and rubbed his eyes.

"You seem to be feeling better today, Mr. Boggs," said Mr. Bigelow. "I'm glad to see it."

"How'd you know my name?" said Franklin.

"We have quite a network of conductors on the underground railroad," said Mr. Bigelow. "South of here a ways one of our lookouts says there is a group of men on the trail of a runaway named Franklin Boggs. The description they gave fits you pretty closely." Franklin stood up. Charity thought Mr. Bigelow was a big man, but Franklin seemed to tower over him. Franklin's face was expressionless, but his eyes were fixed on the white man. "We've diverted them across the lake to New York. You're safe here for now. I'll let you know if they pick up your scent again." A smile flickered across Bea's face. She put her hand to her mouth and cleared her throat. Charity had not seen her smile in months. Franklin looked at her and frowned slightly. "It will be a day or two before we can make arrangements to move you. Meantime, try to get your energy back."

"I'm ready now," said Franklin.

"We're working as fast as we can," said Mr. Bigelow firmly, "but everything must be in order to work smoothly."

"Can you get me to Africa?" said Franklin. His question was followed by a stunned pause. Charity had not thought about going to Africa. It was on the other side of the world—foreign, remote, inaccessible. Her mother had told her that her great-grandparents were kings and queens in West Africa. But she did not speak any native languages, and she did not know their customs. She was afraid they would find her uncivilized.

"I think it can be arranged," said Mr. Bigelow, "but it will take a little more time. Mr. Converse is secretary of the Colonization Society. Thousands of people have gone to Liberia on the west coast of Africa. They've been given land to farm, and I hear cotton grows there as luxuriously as it does in the American south."

"I know things about Africa," said Franklin.

Charity knew about this new country, too, from conversations at Primrose. White men gave it the name from the Latin, *liber*, meaning freedom.

"If you are serious about going, I will consult with Mr. Converse and begin the preparations. I just hope the manhunters give us time to get you on a boat."

"I'm dead serious," said Franklin, looking Mr. Bigelow in the eye.

"In the meantime," said Mr. Bigelow, "the kitchen is stocked with food. If you need anything else, just let me know, and we'll try to accommodate you."

"Tobacco," said Franklin.

"That's easy enough," said Mr. Bigelow.

"And a pipe," said Franklin.

"Are you particular about the type?" said Mr. Bigelow. Charity was amazed at Franklin's demands and at Mr. Bigelow's cheerful compliance. Franklin treated him as if he were a servant, but Mr. Bigelow was unruffled.

"No," said Franklin. "Long as I can smoke it."

"I'll have it sent right down."

Charity jumped in. "What happened to Sunday?"

"She should be in Canada soon," said Mr. Bigelow. "When we have word, we'll tell the jackal who seems to have set up residence in my front yard. Then I hope we won't be bothered with him again." He looked at Charity and changed the subject. "I understand you've been making excursions into Burlington, young lady."

"I . . . Sissy . . ., " began Charity.

"Well, I'd like to offer you an invitation to join Mrs. Bigelow and me for Sunday services at Reverend Young's church. I will guarantee your safety, and Cecilia will be joining us." Charity's eyes widened. She looked at Bea, who avoided her gaze. "Oh, yes," he said, "she asked me to give you this." He held out the black bonnet, which he had been holding behind his back. Sissy must have told him everything. Charity didn't need much time to deliberate. Bea had dug in her heels for now anyway, and going out would pass the time. Then there was Franklin. Charity reached for the bonnet.

"That girl goes out, she'll lead the slave catchers right back to us," said Franklin.

"She will be my guest and leave by the front door," Mr. Bigelow assured him.

"All I been through, I'm not going to have some little girl get me sent right back where I came from." Franklin's voice was softer than usual, but there was an edge of violence in the quiet tone.

"Mr. Boggs," said Mr. Bigelow firmly, "I will do everything in my power to ensure your security. Believe me," he added, "I have nearly as much to lose as you do."

"We've got to trust Mr. Bigelow," said Isaac.

Franklin looked at Bea, who had turned her back. "She's got a mind of her own," Bea said without turning around. "Let her go."

Chapter Fifteen

Charity smoothed her hair down as best she could and nestled the bonnet onto her head. She tied the bow under her chin and followed Mr. Bigelow through the back stairway to a door that opened into the main house. Unlike the airy rooms of Primrose, this New England house was dark and subdued. She felt if she were to speak at all, it would be a whisper, out of respect for some invisible antiquity inhabiting the colorless busts of vacant-eyed men that lorded over the chambers from their thin pedestals.

They walked down a hallway to a sitting room. The doors and the window frames were bare wood stained deep brown. The floors, too, were dark wood, crowned by rugs of reds and golds woven into intricate designs. The chair cushions were rich tapestries, and their arms were carved lions with mouths open in yawning snarls. A heavy-looking desk had claw feet on the ends of the legs, and each balanced uncomfortably on a metal ball. A clock as tall as Mr. Bigelow stood against one wall. The face had roman numerals, and flowers cascaded in an arc above it. It was 10:30. On each side of the clock was a life-sized oil painting, one of a woman, the other of a man. The young woman had a manly face with tubular curls hanging at her temples. There was no passion, no emotion at all in her expression. She held a book in her hand with her thumb marking the place. The man wore black evening clothes, and his stiff posture gave him an air of self-importance. He was not enjoying the floppy-eared dog who was jumping onto his lap. There were other paintings, too, of paddleboats wedged between choppy water and swirling clouds, or sailboats battling storms. It was a gloomy room, except for the tall fireplace, where embers glowed around the andirons.

Sissy and Mrs. Bigelow appeared from a doorway that led to another room. Sissy was wearing a blue dress with a wide pink sash tied at the waist. Her red curls had been tamed by a big pink bow at the nape of her neck. Pink did not favor her. It drained her face of color and made her look transparent.

She greeted Charity with a bear hug that pinned both her arms to her sides. Charity had never seen a person, black or white, who exhibited as much unrestrained affection as this girl did. She stepped back when Sissy let her go.

Mr. Bigelow looked at the tall clock, then checked the watch at the end of the fob attached to his vest and declared that they had better be on their way to church or Reverend Young would start without them. He put on his top hat, tapped it as if snapping it into place, and held the door for Mrs. Bigelow, who led the way, followed by Sissy and then Charity. In front of the house, a man skulked behind the coach. Charity remembered Sheffield's narrow face from Sheriff Barnes' wagon the day before. "Better be on your way or you'll be late for church," said Mr. Bigelow to the man. He scowled and spit on the ground where Mr. Bigelow's lawn would be when the snow was gone, then wiped his bushy mustache with the back of his sleeve. He did not reply, but looked with such loathing at Mr. Bigelow that he completely ignored Charity and Sissy, for which Charity was grateful.

Mr. Bigelow held out his hand to help Charity up onto the high step, as he did with the other ladies. They drove straight up Church Street, Mr. Bigelow complaining that they should walk if they weren't in a hurry and it wasn't so blasted cold, even though Charity thought it was much warmer than the day before. Sissy pointed up College Street to a brown stone building three stories high and said it was Union School, where her classroom was on the third floor. Her teacher, she said, was Miss Joy, who seemed to take extreme displeasure in her students deriving any. She also had a fixation about the conjugation of irregular verbs and considered dangling participles a sign of loose morals. Other than that, said Sissy, she was not a bad teacher.

They were almost to the end of Church Street when they passed Jim Raskin dressed in his Sunday clothes. He was riding a fine-looking horse, much more frisky than the old mare Charity had seen on Saturday. Mr. Bigelow saluted as they passed and said good morning. Jim smiled and tipped his hat.

"Isn't that a new horse Jim is riding?" said Mr. Bigelow.

"I wouldn't be surprised," said Mrs. Bigelow.

"Funny," he said, "it looks uncannily like your young mare, Daisy."

"Yes, it does, doesn't it?" said Mrs. Bigelow. Mr. Bigelow's eyebrows formed question marks, and he tilted his head to look under them at Mrs. Bigelow.

"I didn't know she was for sale," he said.

"She wasn't," she said with a note of finality and focused her eyes straight ahead.

They left the carriage with others in the circular driveway of the church and walked up the stairs to the tall front doors.

Mr. and Mrs. Bigelow greeted friends, while Sissy put her arm around Charity and scurried her around them into the vestibule, where they waited for the adults. Charity looked into the sanctuary. It was an immense room. The walls, ceiling, and supporting pillars were coated with thick white paint. A balcony ran around three walls, and it, too, was painted white. The varnish on the narrow board floor was worn. Two aisles cut passages between the rows of pews and ran to the altar, where a polished mahogany pulpit stood. On a chair behind the pulpit sat Reverend Young, one hand holding a book and the other resting on his knee. A long black robe, shiny like satin, engulfed him from neck to feet. The whole setting felt unnatural. On Sundays at home, services were held in a shed, and wind whistled through the cracks between the barnboards summer and winter. Birds sang, and frogs croaked a throaty percussion.

Mr. and Mrs. Bigelow ushered the girls to an empty pew on the left near the back. An organ must have been above them in the balcony. Charity could not see it, but it droned melodically as they sat down. She could feel the vibrations of the organ in her buttocks and her back as the pew shuddered at its volume. She looked around the huge room, and her eyes were drawn to the tall windows. Outside, the tree limbs were turning crimson as nature's blood rushed into the branches to feed the leaf buds. A fly crawled sluggishly across the glass. It stopped now and then as if puzzled by the clear view of the outside and its inability to gain access to it. Then, in a burst of energy, it buzzed madly in a circle, hitting itself against the pane. Finally, it fell to the sill exhausted, and lay on its back, still. Each time it happened, just as Charity was sure the fly was dead, it flew up with renewed fervor and began the cycle again.

Sissy tugged at her sleeve. She was standing up and motioned for Charity to do the same. The congregation had begun singing a hymn, but the slow bellow of the organ nearly drowned out the voices. It was just as well, thought Charity, since she had never heard the hymn before. Sissy shared a hymnbook with her to follow along. Each note was slow and labored, and the choir drew out the words as if they had some deep, sad significance. Charity stifled a yawn before the end of the first verse. When she realized they were going to sing all five verses, she began to pinch herself to keep her attention focused. She squeezed her eyes shut and opened them, and they began to water, which made her nose run, and she sniffed a few times. Mrs. Bigelow offered her a lace handkerchief and looked at her sympathetically, and she dabbed her cheeks with it. No one clapped or swayed, and there was no indication that the music invoked the spirit of anyone in the congregation except as a funeral might do.

Charity was glad when the sermon began. At least the preaching would keep her awake. Sissy passed her a piece of paper that had the order of service written on it, and she saw that the sermon was titled, "The Eleventh Commandment." Reverend Young told the story of Joseph in the book of Genesis, whose brothers traded him for twenty pieces of silver. His new owners sold him as a slave in Egypt. Generations later an Egyptian pharaoh made slaves of all the Israelites, even those who had been neighbors and friends. They worked until they collapsed, and then they were beaten until they got up and worked some more. Then he told about another Unitarian minister, Ralph Waldo Emerson, who said that what we do to others, we do to ourselves, because we are all part of one perfect spirit. If we bind even one little toe, we feel the pain throughout the whole body. If the binding is too tight, the whole being grows sick and could even die. So it is with slavery, he said. The skin may have a different hue, but we are all partners in the divine plan.

When he was finished there was a momentary silence. Charity looked around. One or two heads were nodding sleepily, and the rest seemed to be in a hypnotic trance. She felt sorry for Reverend Young then, and thought how disappointed he must be not to have affected at least one member of his audience, besides herself. She thought perhaps if she could just break the ice by calling out "Amen," others would join in. But she knew better than to risk being noticed. She turned toward Sissy, who was drawing tulips on the order of service.

When the organ boomed the recessional, Reverend Young hurried down an aisle to the back of the church to greet the congregation, and Charity and Sissy got ready to leave.

"Where's your mother?" said Charity.

"She's in the parlor getting things ready for the coffee hour," said Sissy. "She half listens to the sermon through the wall, but Father usually gives her a preview of the service anyway." She pushed Charity down the aisle. "Come on. We have a lot to do today."

Chapter Sixteen

Reverend Young beamed. "Charity, welcome to our church." He squeezed her hand. "Did you enjoy the sermon?"

"Yes, very much," said Charity. She wanted to add that she seemed to be the only one who did, but she didn't want to hurt his feelings.

"I'm glad you have become Cecilia's friend," he said. "Cecilia, bring Charity home for dinner this afternoon."

"But Father," protested Sissy, "I promised Tess we'd come for a party at the lake." People were pressing behind them and Sissy yelled the last information over her shoulder as she and Charity trotted down the steps.

They said good-bye to Mr. and Mrs. Bigelow, who were on their way to the parlor to attend the coffee. At the end of the walkway, the girls paused to let a carriage pass down Pearl Street.

"Well, if it isn't the preacher's daughter," said a voice on Sissy's right. Willy Peck was leaning against a lamppost. His frock coat was pinned open by his hand, which was stuck into his pants pocket. The other was planted firmly on a hip. A wide bow tie was askew at his neck, and his threadlike mouth quivered in a tentative smirk. Sissy ignored him.

"Hello, Marie," he said. "Won't you give me a civil word, at least?" Charity tugged at the brim of her bonnet.

"Hey, where's that hatpin I gave you yesterday? You should show off that pretty face." He reached over and touched Charity's cheek with the backs of his fingers. She jerked away from him.

"Leave her alone, Willy," said Sissy.

"Not jealous, are you, Sissy?"

Sissy looked up the street. Another carriage was coming.

"So, you been to hear your daddy sermonizing about the evils of slavery again?" he said.

"Shut your mouth, Willy," said Sissy. The girls crossed Pearl Street and headed down Church Street. Willy crossed with them, walking sideways so he could continue his taunting. "It's your father who should shut his, you little strumpet, his and every one of his other slave-lovers'."

"I wouldn't be so quick to talk, Willy," said Sissy. "Your father is good friends with my father."

"My father doesn't know what's good for him. You bring those black-faced beggars up here and pretty soon they'll be taking our jobs away from us. Then they'll be wanting to vote so they can start telling us what to do. Pretty soon the whole country will be run by a bunch of baboons. Only thing they're good for is the reward money. I'd like to catch me a runaway. I'd turn him in quicker than you can spit."

Sissy stopped and turned toward Willy. She curled her hands into fists and thrust them onto her hips, elbows out. "Now, look here, Mr. Smart-mouth," she said. "You don't have the sense God gave a worm. It wouldn't hurt you to listen to what my father has to say."

"I know what he has to say," said Willy, "and I know it doesn't amount to a pile of horse plop. There's going to be a war over these Negroes, and they aren't worth the blood that's going to be shed for them. By the time I'm seventeen, the South will have its own army, and I'll be one of the first to join. You won't see me fighting for the pigeon-hearted Northerners. Only ones up here who have any sense are the ones who want to send them back where they came from."

"They're Americans, just like you, Willy. They were born in America."

"Then why don't they look American?" he said.

"You don't look American, either," said Sissy. "If you did, you'd be out west eating buffalo meat and fighting for your land. Maybe we should send you back to England or whatever country has the misfortune of claiming you. Good-bye, Willy." Sissy started to walk away, and Charity fell into step beside her.

'Wait a minute," he said. "Marie, don't let that slave-loving preacher and his daughter put ugly ideas into your head. Hey, if you come by the store tomorrow, I'll treat you to root beer at Abraham's. What do you say?"

Sissy stopped and put an arm around Charity's shoulders. She looked up at Willy.

"Let's get something straight, Willy," she said. "Marie speaks French. If she understood everything you've said, she would find you utterly distasteful, I'm sure."

"Oh yeah? Well, how come I haven't heard her say anything in French yet?"

"I don't think the appropriate insult exists in the language of romance, but maybe she can come up with something. Marie?" said Sissy. Charity's mind was whirling to think of a French expression from the literature she had read. She drew a blank.

92

"She's very shy, Willy, and you have her all flustered," said Sissy.

"Will!" A man yelled from the other side of Church Street. "Get on down to the store and help unload that wagon."

"But, Dad," Willy protested, "it's Sunday."

"Don't matter, boy," he said. "Work's got to be done."

"Adieu," said Charity. She wasn't sure where the word came from—maybe it was in a poem she had read.

"Well, what do you know," said Willy. The girls turned and left him standing on the street, gawking after them. "Don't forget the root beer, Marie," he called.

"Willy Peck is the incarnation of Satan himself," said Sissy. "Let's go. Tess is probably waiting for us by now."

The girls hurried to the little house on Pine Street. Tess had packed a basket of food and was bundling up Lida when they arrived.

"I don't think she'll be needing all those clothes," said Sissy. "It's warmed up today. Icicles were dripping from the roof of the church. In fact, we may have to go for a swim to cool off." They all laughed together, and Lida clapped her hands.

"Where's Nate?" asked Charity.

"He's at work. Sunday is one of the busiest days at the restaurant," said Tess. "The crowd comes in right after church to have dinner. And Mr. Wiggins—that's his boss—said he heard that the train coming in from Washington is carrying a full load. He had to go in earlier than usual today."

"So I guess it will be just us girls, right Lida?" said Sissy. She picked up Lida and whirled her around in a circle, her little feet flying out behind her. Lida giggled gleefully.

The basket was heavy, and Sissy and Charity each took a handle and carried it together out the door and down toward the lake. Lida wanted to walk, but she could not keep up, and Tess carried her most of the way.

They found a spot in the sun where a rocky ledge sheltered them from the wind, and the girls set down the lunch. The air was chilly, but the sun felt wonderful. A few skaters were out on the lake, but the surface of the ice had softened since the day before, and only the older children were skating. They seemed to be gliding less and falling more, Charity thought. The fishing shanties were still there and several fishermen angled through their augured holes, but there were no horses or wagons on the ice today.

Sissy and Charity dragged a wooden log to the picnic site to sit on, and Tess handed out sandwiches wrapped in stiff white paper.

"I hope you like smoked meat, Charity," said Tess.

"I've never had it," said Charity.

"You'd better get used to it." Tess laughed. "The Canadians eat it all the time."

Charity bit into the sandwich and found it delicious. It was spicy and tasted as if it had been cooked over a wood fire.

"Oh, I forgot glasses," said Tess. "We'll have to be a little primitive today." She passed around a bottle filled with apple cider, and each of the girls took a drink. Lida tried to imitate the big girls, but turned the bottle up too fast and spilled cider down the front of her coat. Sissy grabbed a cloth that Tess had brought and wiped it off before it soaked in. Then she helped Lida drink until she was satisfied.

When they had finished their sandwiches, the girls folded the paper, and Tess put it back into the basket.

"Now for dessert," she said. She took three tin bowls from the basket and gave one to each girl. Charity looked at hers and wondered what kind of dessert came in an empty bowl. Then Tess took out a jar labeled "sour pickles" and a bag that was stained with greasy spots. "Sissy, you'd better show Charity what to do," she said.

94

"Follow us," said Sissy. Holding her bowl, she picked up Lida, who had hers clenched in both fists, and walked away from where they had been sitting. She put Lida down and began to clear away the top layer of dingy snow from an area that had not been disturbed by footprints. She dug down to where the snow was still fresh and white. "Fill your bowl here," she said to Charity. Charity wondered why, if she was going to eat snow, she had to put it into a bowl instead of just scooping it with her hands. She thought maybe this was some strange New England custom, and she went along with it good-naturedly.

They brought the bowls back to Tess. She had taken another jar from the basket, this one containing a thick brown liquid. She removed the lid, and steam rose from the contents. "Bring your bowl here, Lida," she said. Sissy helped Lida steady her bowl under the jar while her mother poured some of the brown substance onto the snow. Charity thought the warm liquid would melt the snow, but as soon as it touched the cold, it began to solidify.

"We call this sugar-on-snow," said Sissy. "It's the first maple syrup of the season."

"Snow," said Lida. Sissy cleaned off a stick for Lida to use to lift the maple sugar to her mouth. Then Tess poured the syrup onto Charity's snow and then onto Sissy's.

"You'd better get some, too, Tess," said Charity.

"Don't worry," said Tess. "I'll have to finish Lida's."

"What's the other stuff for?" said Charity.

"Just wait," said Sissy. "Keep eating."

Charity had never tasted anything as sweet as this maple sugar, but soon she felt like she couldn't take another bite. The sweetness hurt her teeth and caused a pain in her head. "I can't eat any more," she said.

"Then it's time for a pickle," said Sissy. "Here. Bite into this." She handed Charity a little cucumber from the jar.

Charity hesitantly took a bite and prepared to pucker. She was surprised when it didn't taste sour at all. Instead, it seemed to neutralize the sweetness and made her hungry for more maple sugar.

"Now have one of these," said Tess, and she handed her the bag, which was full of freshly made doughnuts. Charity took one.

"What do these do?" asked Charity.

"They just taste good," said Sissy. "And it's tradition."

"Gooood," said Lida, grinning. Now she was chewing on a doughnut. Brown maple coated her mouth, and a piece of partially chewed pickle was hanging off the front of her coat.

"It's hard to believe this is her first sugar-on-snow party, isn't it?" said Tess.

"She's a born Vermonter," said Sissy.

They all laughed and ate, and Charity could not remember when she had felt so full. It began to cloud up, but that didn't lessen her enjoyment of the day. She wished Bea could be there to share the good time, and she tried to remember every detail so she could tell her about it when she got back.

After a while the clouds completely blocked the sun, and a damp chill settled in. Charity said that she should go back to the ell to make sure Bea was all right.

"First," said Sissy, "come slide on the ice with Lida and me. You come, too, Tess."

"Naw," said Tess. "You young folks go have fun. I'll just clean up here."

Sissy put Lida on her shoulders, one leg on each side of her neck. She held onto Lida's knees and slipped onto the ice. Charity followed them down, and they skated in circles around each other. Lida was squealing with delight.

"Mind if I join in, ladies?" It was Willy Peck.

"I thought you had work to do," said Sissy.

"Finished it."

"Well, you just find somewhere else to skate."

"When did you buy Lake Champlain?"

"We were here first, Willy," said Sissy, and she shoved him. He stumbled backwards, lost his footing on the ice, and fell sprawling on his backside. Lida clapped.

"Do again, Sis-sis," she said. Sissy laughed out loud.

"I'll get you, you little harlot," grated Willy, his angelic face twisted into a snarl. He managed to get to his feet, gain his balance, and lunge for Sissy. She spun out of his grasp and ran toward the breakwater, Lida bouncing on her shoulders, with Willy close behind.

"Sissy!" yelled Tess from the shore. "Look out for Lida."

Charity stood for a minute watching the three diminish in size as they got farther out. Her temples began to pulsate, and she sensed danger. She started after them but lost her footing and fell onto one knee. The surface of the ice was wet, and it quickly soaked into her skirt. She struggled to her feet and began to run again, half jogging and half sliding. When Charity switched her attention from her feet to Sissy and Lida, Sissy had run past the skaters and the fishermen and was about halfway to the breakwater. Willy was cursing and sliding awkwardly behind them. Charity tried to increase her speed, but she couldn't seem to reduce the distance between them. She could hear the playful chatter of the skaters, and she caught isolated words of the fishermen's terse conversations.

When she reached the crack where the black ice began, she saw that it had widened, and she had to jump over it in order to clear it. She nearly lost her balance again, but managed to steady herself. She looked up to see that Sissy and Lida were almost to the breakwater, and Willy was lagging farther behind.

Charity was breathing hard and was beginning to sweat. She loosened the collar of her shirt and wiped her forehead with the back of her hand. Then she heard a scream. She looked up just in time to see Sissy disappear through the ice. Lida fell off her shoulders and thumped onto the ice on her back, then started to cry loudly. Willy stopped twenty feet from the hole as if his feet had suddenly frozen to the ice. His face was ashen, and his eyes were wide with panic. Charity ran past him and toward Lida as fast as she could. The brim of the bonnet kept blowing down into her face, and she tore it off and threw it to the side. Lida was standing up and crying, "Sis-sis, Sis-sis." She was starting to toddle toward the hole where Sissy had fallen in. Charity called to her.

"Lida! Lida, honey, come here," she said.

"Sis-sis, Sis-sis," cried Lida.

"It's okay, honey. Come to Charity." Lida turned and slowly walked toward Charity. Just as Charity was able to grab Lida, Tess appeared somehow on the ice next to her, and Charity thought she must have flown over it to get there so quickly. She gave Lida to Tess and turned to look for Sissy.

"Marie!" yelled Willy. "Marie, come back. You'll go through, too."

But Charity didn't hear him. She was encased in complete silence. The sky was a metallic gray, and the mountains seemed to glow with a phosphorescence. The air was perfectly still, and every nerve in her body was vibrating. Then she heard a drum. She thought at first it was the thumping of her heart, but its beat was irregular, sometimes loud, sometimes soft. She felt it throb through her veins, and every impact of hand on drum increased the knowledge of what she had to do. There was no fear then, only determination.

Charity dropped onto her stomach and inched herself toward the gap. She could see water splashing up around the hole, and she thought she heard a choking sound.

"Sissy!" she yelled. "Can you hear me? Sissy! Answer me!"

"Yes," said Sissy, coughing. "Help!"

"Willy!" said Charity. "The bonnet. Get the bonnet." Willy hesitated. "Willy!" yelled Charity again. "Throw me the bonnet. Hurry!" Slowly Willy inched toward the bonnet. Finally he reached it and tossed it to Charity. She slid on her belly closer and closer to the hole. The ice near the breakwater was beginning to break up into chunks, and Charity knew that at any instant it could give way beneath her.

"Sissy!" she called. "I'm going to throw you the bonnet. I want you to grab it. All right?" Sissy coughed, and then there was silence. "Sissy!"

"Yes," she managed weakly.

"Here it comes," said Charity. "Grab it now." She threw the bonnet into the cavity, holding onto the ties until she felt them tense in her hands. "I'm going to pull you up now. Hold on tight." She dug her toes into the ice and tried to push her body away from the opening. But Sissy, wet and panicky, weighed more than she did, and Charity felt herself slipping toward her. She pulled the sashes, hand over hand, until Sissy's upstretched arm was right in front of her. She could see Sissy's red hair floating on the surface just beneath her, and the icy water splashed up onto her face. Just as the watery mouth threatened to devour them both, Charity felt a pair of hands grasp her ankles, and she began to slide backward, away from the hole. She clamped onto Sissy's wrist with both hands until she saw the dripping head emerge from the ice. A man's big hand pulled her up and dragged them both away from the gaping tear.

Near the shore, a crowd had gathered, and several people carried Sissy back to land, where Tess was waiting with Lida. Someone appeared with a blanket and put it around Sissy's shoulders. Tess told a man who Sissy's father was and where she lived. A wagon appeared. Tess helped load Sissy onto it, and then she and Lida got on, too. Charity stood and watched them disappear up the hill.

Chapter Seventeen

"Is this yours?" A little boy was looking up at Charity. One front tooth was missing. He was holding a soggy black bonnet out to her.

"I guess it is," she said and took the hat from him.

She found the picnic basket on the shore and tried to pick it up, but it was too heavy to move by herself. The strength had drained from her limbs, and she sat down on the log to rest. Her clothes were damp, and strings of hair were sticking to her face. The wind was picking up, and she shivered.

"You okay?" One of the fishermen was beside her. When Charity tried to stand, he took her elbow and helped her to her feet. She recognized the broad hands. He had dragged Sissy and her to safety.

"Dern fool thing running all the way out there in this thaw," he said "Got to stay close to shore when she's starting to thin. Still, that was a brave thing you done. Girl woulda died pretty quick in that cold water. Lucky you didn't go in yourself." He hesitated awkwardly. Then he said, "Need any help gettin' home?" She shook her head.

"You the one that saved the girl?" a woman asked. People had gathered around, staring at Charity, and she began backing away. Her disguise, the rumpled bonnet, was useless now—it flapped in the wind as it dangled from her hand. She had to get back to the ell, and she looked around for a way to escape. A raindrop hit her in the face, then another, then a gust of wind brought a wave of cold rain. The crowd broke up and ran for cover. Charity shielded her head with the crumpled bonnet and paused to look out at the hole in the lake. Then she turned and started walking up the hill. This was not the way she wanted to say good-bye to Sissy, but she knew it would be best to leave for Canada as soon as possible.

Charity headed down Church Street, and by now she was drenched. She ducked inside a carriage house to get out of the rain for a minute, straightened her skirt, and brushed the water off her coat.

"Marie!" She looked around to see Willy Peck standing close behind her, his wet hair clinging to his forehead. He was breathing heavily, and his body was tensed. In all the confusion, she had forgotten about him.

"You and Sissy tried to make a fool out of me, didn't you? I heard you talking to her, and it wasn't French words you were using. Where'd you really come from—and you'd better tell me the truth this time." He was pointing a finger at her, threatening her.

Anger surged through Charity. She was tired of games. She wanted to swat this obnoxious white boy like a bothersome mosquito.

"You want the truth, Willy? You're right—I'm not from Canada. I'm black, Negro, African. I'm one of those baboons,

102

those black-faced beggars you detest so. What do you think, Willy? You want your hatpin back now?"

Willy lunged at her, knocking her to the ground. His forearm was across her chest, pinning her down. With his other hand, he slapped her sharply across the face. He was yelling at her, and his breath smelled of rotting apples. She struggled under his weight, but could only get one hand free. When his hand went back again, she felt for her coat lapel, found the brass knob, and pulled the hatpin out. Clenching it in her fist, she drew it back over her head and thrust it forward, aiming for Willy's eye. He threw his head back, and the hatpin entered his mouth, punctured his tongue, and plunged still deeper, until its sharp tip broke through the skin under his chin. He rolled off her and fell back onto the floor, blood spurting from his mouth. He grabbed for his throat, his cheeks, searching blindly for the intruder, rolling in pain. Finally he was silent, except for the dull thud of his feet kicking wildly on the ground. Charity left him there and ran toward the Bigelow house.

In the distance she could see the narrow-faced Sheffield, his shoulders hunched against the rain, pacing anxiously in front of the house. Charity put her head down and crossed the street, heading for the driveway. But she could not risk having him follow her to the back entrance of the ell. On second thought, she marched up to the Bigelow's front door and knocked loudly, praying that someone who knew her would answer.

The door opened, and a woman she had never seen before dressed in a servant's uniform stood before her.

"Good Lord, child, what happened to you?" she said. Charity burst past her, turned and stood in the foyer.

"Close the door . . . please," she said. "I need to see Mrs. Bigelow at once." The woman closed the door slowly.

"Mrs. Bigelow is not home. Stay right here. Let me get you a towel."

When she left the room, Charity peeked out the window and saw that Sheffield was still staring at the front door. She took off her shoes and followed the path through the house that led to the cellar stairway. Fortunately, the door was not locked, and she descended the stairs to the alcove.

"Bea, it's me—Charity," she called through the panel. The wall slid open, and Charity went in, collapsing onto her bed. Bea helped her out of her muddy clothes and wiped her face.

"You're bleeding," said Bea. "What happened?" Charity told her about Sissy falling through the ice, and the rescue, but she left out the part about Willy Peck. She didn't regret what she'd done, but she wasn't asking for trouble, either. Bea got her into dry clothes and made her a cup of hot tea. George came and sat by her, and Isaac pulled up a chair. Franklin sat across the room on his cot, leaning his back against the wall and smoking a new pipe. Charity told them about the slave catcher outside the Bigelow house.

"Are they gonna find us and take us back?" said George.

"No, son," said Isaac. "He's just sniffing around, looking for Sunday, and she's already gone to freedom. He's no threat to us."

"I don't feel too easy about it, just the same," said Franklin. "We going to have to find a way to push things along. I got to think about what we're going to do."

Charity wondered what he meant by "we," but she didn't have the strength to pursue the question. A dull ache of apprehension was creeping up through her bones and taking hold of her brain.

"Will you teach me to read some more tonight, Charity?" asked George.

"Maybe in a little while, George. Let me just rest for a few minutes, and then we'll see."

Chapter Eighteen

When Charity tried to raise her head to get out of bed, a sharp pain pierced her neck. She lay back down. She tried to turn onto her side, and pain stabbed her between the shoulder blades and shot up into the back of her head. She lifted her arms to her forehead. They felt like heavy sandbags. She lay still and tried moving other parts of her body, but there were few places where she did not ache. She felt like a machine that had been left out in the rain to rust, and now she needed a good oiling. Her right hand hurt more than anywhere else, and, when she looked at it, she saw that a piece of clean cotton had been wrapped around it. Two dots of red had oozed through the bandage over the back of her fingers. It took a few minutes for the events of the previous day to come back to her. She didn't remember hurting her hand. It was fine when she pulled Sissy from the water, and she hadn't injured it on the way home. Then she remembered Willy Peck and the hatpin sticking through his tongue. His teeth must have scraped her knuckles when she drove it into his mouth. She wondered why she hadn't noticed.

She exhaled a low moan. Bea came over, sat on the edge of the bed, and smoothed the hair from Charity's face.

"You feeling poorly?" asked Bea.

"Yes," said Charity. "I feel like I have a toothache all over my body." Bea laughed out loud. For the second time in two days, Bea was good-natured, and Charity was struck by how strange it was to see her happy. Her appearance changed when she smiled. Her eyes sparkled, her cheeks widened, and her whole face brightened. Charity liked seeing her this way.

"You had a rough day yesterday, sister. You better just stay in bed and take it easy today," said Bea. Charity was in no condition to argue with her.

She watched Bea gather some wrappings and a bowl of water, and take them to Franklin's cot. She began to change his bandages without awakening him. Charity was sure he would jump when she touched him because he had been so skittish two days before, but he just turned his head toward Bea and looked up at her. And then he smiled, a slow, lazy smile. And Bea smiled back at him. When she was finished, she ran her hand gently over his hair and let it rest at the top of his head for a minute. All this time neither of them said a word to each other, but Charity felt like they were speaking just the same, only in a language she couldn't understand. She fell asleep again and knew nothing until afternoon, when Bea woke her with a bowl of hot soup.

Bea fixed her pillows and made it more comfortable for her to sit up to eat. Her bandaged hand was clumsy with the spoon, so Bea took it and ladled the hot broth into her mouth. Franklin appeared to be sleeping, and Isaac was reading to George. Now was the time for Charity to ask Bea the questions that had been churning inside her.

"Bea, what did Franklin mean about my father owning slaves? Does he know what he's talking about?"

Bea put the soup bowl down. She folded her hands in her lap and looked at the floor. She chewed gently on her bottom lip. Charity was used to Bea's long silences. She knew that what followed would be carefully measured.

"When you were born, I was so happy to have me a little sister. You were like a little baby doll I always wanted. And Mama, she was crazy about you, too. You were so pretty, with skin like . . . "

Charity was suddenly afraid to ask the next question, but she had come this far, and she felt she couldn't turn back. "Bea, why is my skin so much lighter than yours? Mama is dark, and so is Daddy."

Bea reached over and curled a strand of Charity's hair around her finger. "I knew someday you would ask these questions, sister, but I didn't think it would be this hard to answer them." She paused again, but Charity kept quiet, and after a moment she continued. "Slavery takes advantage of people in lots of ways. None of it is pleasant. Men are forced to do a white man's work without pay or reward. Women are forced to do things, too . . . other things."

"Bea, what are you saying?" Charity searched her sister's face for an answer. Ages later, Bea began again.

"Sister, you and I come from the same mother, but we have different fathers."

"What do you mean? Mama had two men? Who was there besides Daddy?" Charity knew the answer, but she wanted Bea to confirm it.

"Master Pearson."

"Oh, God," said Charity. She covered her face with her hands.

"That's why Daddy was always so mean to you. It wasn't your fault. Every time he looked at you, he saw his white master, and his grief just festered inside him until it exploded."

Charity understood everything now, why Master Pearson brought her to the big house, why his wife whipped her, why white people mistook her for one of them. She wondered if Bethy knew. Bethy, her half sister. But Bea was her half sister too. She studied Bea's face, the strong, tranquil face of the only family she had left.

"Where do I belong, Bea?" said Charity. "In here with you or out there with them?" Bea put her arms around Charity.

"You belong right here with me. You're my flesh and my blood, and don't you ever forget it." Bea held Charity for a few minutes and then she took a deep breath. "There's more, sister, and while I'm telling it, I might as well tell it all." She swallowed and began again. "Master Pearson liked his women to be young. He liked to be the first one, but Mama outsmarted him and had me before he could get to her. But he had his way with her anyway. Then when I got older, he started looking at me. He'd come up to me and say things a man shouldn't say to a woman unless he has some evil in him. And that white man is evil, all right. He said he was saving me for just the right time, and I'd better be ready. I swear I could have run away, but I didn't want to leave you, and I wanted to make sure we could run without being caught."

"Who was that man who was waiting for us with the wagon that night?" asked Charity.

"His name is John Morris. He owns the farm down the road from Primrose. He was working some deal with Master Pearson, and he made regular visits. Don't you ever remember seeing him?" Charity shook her head. "He was friendly, and he took an interest in me, asking after my health and such. Sometimes he brought Polly, one of his slaves, and we got to be friends. One time I asked Master Pearson if I could visit Polly on a Sunday afternoon. Do you remember before we left Virginia when I went off that day? He said I could if I was back an hour before nightfall, or he'd come after me himself. Well, I went to John's house and told him that I wanted to get free, and I wanted to take you with me. He made a bargain with me that day."

"What was the bargain, Bea?" asked Charity.

"His wife is bedridden. She's real sickly. And he said he was lonely. He said he promised to help us . . ." Bea rubbed the back of one hand with the other and stared across the room at the blanket on the wall. Finally, she said, ". . . if I'd do something for him." Bea sighed. "He kept his promise."

"Did you keep yours?" said Charity.

"I was willing to do anything to get away from Primrose."

This was the worst horror of slavery, wounding where scars were not visible. And then a thought began to form, growing bigger by the second until Charity could no longer bear its weight. Bea's sick spells, her fatigue, her moodiness, all made sense now.

"Bea, you're going to have his baby, aren't you?"

"What's done is done. Anyway, my baby's not going to be born a slave," Bea said. "I'm African, and it's going to be African." She looked at Charity. "We're going with Franklin."

"Bea, I'm not going to Africa." Charity had heard enough. She was sure Bea was mad. "And neither are you. We can take care of the baby fine ourselves in Canada. And then, when slavery ends, we can come back across the border to America."

"There'll never be an end to slavery," said Franklin. "At least not in this country. And Canada's just another white man's land. In Liberia we'll make our own laws, and won't be no slave hunters to take us back, ever."

"Bea," Charity pleaded, "we're almost there. I can smell the air of freedom from here. Can't you, Bea?" But Bea's jaw was set—she wasn't listening.

Chapter Nineteen

"You'll see," said Franklin. "Liberia has sandy beaches and mountains taller than you ever saw, and enough rain to grow healthy crops. We won't ever have to pick cotton again. We can harvest our own rubber trees. Rubber makes good money anywhere in the world."

"How do you know all this, Franklin? You've never been to Africa," said Charity.

"No, but I listen to people who been there. I worked with a man named Taa-tii. He was from Mali, north of Liberia. He was rich when he lived there. When he came to America, he wore gold necklaces, and had rings on every finger and fine clothes."

"Then what was he doing slaving with you?" said Charity.

"He came here of his free will to see what he had heard about the New World. He walked with his head high through the streets of New York. One day a man grabbed him. Took his gold and put him in chains. When he was in Mali, he was a businessman. In America, he was just a piece of meat for the white man to make money off."

"What happened to him?" asked Bea.

"I guess he's still on that plantation," said Franklin. "Never saw his family again. Maybe we'll see him back in Africa someday."

Charity closed her eyes. She was not in a mood to argue about going to Africa. Franklin had a mind-hold on Bea, and Charity would have to come up with some strong medicine to break it. Maybe she would talk to Mr. Bigelow about leaving in the night the way Sunday had. Bea would be happy after they were in Canada. And having a little sister like Lida would be fun. Bea would see. It would all work out. Charity would make sure of it.

She drifted off to sleep again. When she awoke the light had faded. She thought she heard thunder rumbling nearby. Or perhaps it was rain beating heavily on the roof. Then she remembered she was in a cellar. When she opened her eyes, she saw George dancing in the center of the room. His head was bobbing up and down, and he was lifting his feet like he was marching. His hips were moving from side to side, and his arms were twitching. Isaac was standing in one place, but he was swaying from foot to foot, and his head, too, was keeping time. Charity could feel the vibration all through her body. She struggled to pivot her head to see where the beat was coming from, but her neck still hurt. She turned her shoulders so her head would not move in isolation. It was Franklin. He was holding a pot upside down between his knees and drumming his fingertips gently on the bottom. The movement of his hands did not seem to hurt his shoulder. He was not drumming hard—each stroke was like a caress, making a hollow sound, like an echo. It was hard to tell if Franklin was drumming to George's dance or George was dancing to Franklin's drum. They were synchronized with each other.

Suddenly Franklin stopped. "Hey, little sister," he said. "Get up and dance."

"Franklin," said Charity, "where did you learn to drum like that?"

"From Taa-tii. In Mali he played a drum made from goatskin stretched across a hollowed-out log. On the plantation Taa-tii made one from cowhide. Played it to make our work lighter. We worked and sang to the drum, and we picked more cotton. He taught me to play it, too. Come on. Try it."

"I hurt too much to move, much less dance," said Charity.

"That's the point," he said. "Drums got a healing power. In Africa, when you're sick, you dance the bad spirits away. When you're still, they feed on you. Got to sweat and let them run on out."

"I don't know how to dance," said Charity.

"Anybody can dance," said Franklin. "You just listen to the drum and do what it tells you. See? George is doing it." He started to drum again, and George broke into dance. His mouth was open in a wide smile, and he looked like he was letting loose all the energy he had been holding in the last few days.

Charity struggled to get out of bed. Bea helped her get up. She stood and stretched her arms out to the sides.

"Bea, you dance, too," said Franklin. "That baby's got to get used to hearing drumming. A little swaying will put him right to sleep. This is a lullaby for African babies."

Bea stood at first and just listened to Franklin's hands on the pot. Then the beat seemed to start at the top of her head and flow down through her body. She rolled her head from side to side, and raised and lowered her shoulders. Her rib cage started rising and falling, and her hips rotated back and forth. At last she got her legs and feet into the rhythm, and she was dancing. Her body moved fluidly, each part working separately and together at the same time. Her eyes were fixed on Franklin's. They were like two children on a seesaw, balancing their weight against each other.

The seduction of the drum pulled Charity onto the floor almost against her will. The first movements intensified her aches, but the more she danced, the more limber she became. The drum's throb massaged her sore muscles. The beat settled in her hips, the movement radiating out from the center of her body. It felt good, and she forgot the twinges that had sent her to bed.

Each one was dancing a different dance, but they were all dancing to the same rhythm, like Reverend Young said yesterday about all people being part of one whole. Charity forgot to hate her master-father and his spoiled daughter, Bethy. She forgot about Franklin's plan to take Bea to Liberia. She forgot she was a fugitive. There was only the drum and her body moving to it. It was the oil that lubricated her rusty gears. She wanted to suspend time and dance forever.

The knock on the wall panel was faint at first. Then it sounded louder, breaking the pattern of Franklin's drumming. Charity's feet stopped with the drum, and her body went rigid. The sudden silence telescoped her back into the reality of the cellar, but the drum stayed in her head, like the taste of a sweet that lingers on the tongue long after it has passed through the mouth.

Isaac opened the panel for Reverend Young. He seemed confused, as if he had intruded on a ritual whose meaning was beyond his comprehension.

"Did you hear from the outside?" Isaac asked. Charity had not been aware of how loud the drumming was. It had pushed all thoughts from her head.

"Hear what?" said Reverend Young.

"We were making some noise, sir," said Isaac.

"No, I heard nothing," said Reverend Young. "I came because of my daughter. She fell through the ice yesterday. She might have drowned, but Charity pulled her out. I came to thank you, Charity. Mrs. Young and I are deeply indebted to you."

"How is she?" asked Charity.

"She should be fine tomorrow," said Reverend Young. "She rested at home from school today." There was a strained silence. He cleared his throat and began again. "Her friend, Willy Peck, however, has had less fortune. He was attacked by someone with—of all things—a hatpin. I don't suppose you'd know anything about it, would you?" Charity stared dumbly at the minister. "No, I didn't think so. Anyway, he'll be fine, but it will be a while before he's able to tell us what happened. In the meantime, Mrs. Young and I would like to repay you somehow. Would you consider staying with us until you leave town? You'll be more comfortable, and Cecilia would like your company."

There was another silence, and Charity looked at Bea. "Of course, your sister may come, too," he added quickly.

This was the opportunity she needed to get Bea away from Franklin and make her forget about going to Africa. "Yes," said Charity. "We'd like that."

"Good, good," said Reverend Young. "Then I will tell Cecilia and Mrs. Young that you'll be coming."

"No," said Bea. "We're not going anywhere with you. Everything we need is here."

"No need to decide now," said Reverend Young nervously. "Discuss it, and I'll come back tomorrow." He turned to go, and then, as if he remembered something, turned again. "And Charity, I understand that you have become acquainted with Nate and Tess Roberts."

"Yes," said Charity. "And Lida."

"Then you should know that Nate has left for Canada. Mr. Bigelow is driving him to the border right now."

"But why?" said Charity.

"He was waiting our table at the Lake House this noon. I was having lunch with Simon Wires. Apparently Nate's former owner came in on yesterday's train. He must have gotten word somehow that Nate was in Burlington. He sat down at a table next to ours, and when Nate came from the kitchen with a plate of food, he stopped in the doorway. The man was studying the menu, and I don't think he saw Nate, but when Nate saw him he dropped the tray and ran back into the kitchen. He left through the back door and went to Mr. Bigelow's office at the *Daily News*. Mr. Bigelow called for his carriage right then to drive Nate to safety. When he returns tomorrow, he'll gather Nate's belongings from Tess and send them to him."

"What about Tess and Lida?" asked Charity.

"I've just come from talking to Tess. She's making herself ready to join him in a day or two. Mr. Bigelow and I will have to sell their house and send the money and the rest of their possessions to them in Canada."

"You mean they won't be back?" asked Charity.

"Not as long as slavery is allowed. Nobody's safe until we settle this—one way or another."

"Does Sissy know?"

"Cecilia has not been told because, as you know, she is very close with Tess and Lida, and she has already had one severe shock. I think it might be best to tell her after Tess and Lida have gone. But I wanted you to know because of what you've done for us."

"We've got to do something. How can we just sit here?" said Charity.

"I'm afraid there's nothing we can do. Ever since Dred Scott lost his case in the Supreme Court, a slave is considered the possession of his master, even if he is in a free state. Nate's only hope was to get to Canada. I'm worried about Tess, though. I'm not sure she has the strength to travel that distance alone with Lida. She was quite upset when she found out about Nate."

Isaac spoke up. "Let me go with them, Reverend. I've been waiting my turn here anyway. I can help with her bags and make sure she's safe on the way."

Reverend Young rubbed his chin. "I think that will work, Isaac," he said.

"What about George?" said Charity.

George looked helpless, and Charity put an arm around him.

"We'll take care of George," said Franklin.

"I'll tell Mr. Bigelow about the plan," said Reverend Young.

"You just give me the word, Reverend, and I'll be ready," said Isaac.

"Good. And Charity . . . " Reverend Young put his hands on Charity's shoulders and looked into her eyes. "You'd better not take any more chances with adventures outdoors. Willy Peck is dangerous—to all of us. And one more thing." He squeezed her shoulders. "That man named Hendrick was at the restaurant, too, asking about Bea and you." He released her and stepped toward the opening in the wall. "You may need to move fast. Best gather your things together just in case."

Chapter Twenty

Tess couldn't leave without Sissy having a chance to say good-bye. Charity knew she had to do something.

The next morning she looked for the black bonnet. She had dropped it on the floor when she came in the night before last. She got down on her hands and knees and searched under the bed. It was there, crumpled into a lump and still slightly wet. She tried to press the brim flat with her hands, but it seemed to have a mind of its own. She set a pot of water to boil on the stove, and when the steam rose from it, she held the hat over the pot to soften the wrinkles. She looked at her reflection in the metal pot and saw that her hair was sticking out like straw on a scarecrow.

"Bea," she said. "Can you fix my hair?"

"No," said Bea. "You're old enough to do it yourself."

"But I don't know how."

"Then it's time you learned." Bea added, "Oh, I forgot. Sunday left you this." It was a package wrapped in a piece of oilcloth. Charity took it from her sister and ran her hand over the slick surface of the paper. It was a little larger than a letter and somewhat thicker. She opened it quickly, and inside was a hair comb, carved from light-colored wood. There were five teeth with wide spaces between them. It would be able to comb through tangles without causing much pain. Under the comb was a small hand mirror.

"Sunday said she would get new ones when she got to freedom. I guess she thought you needed them more than she did," said Bea.

Charity held up the mirror and looked at herself. She looked younger than she thought. She felt old, sometimes older than Bea. Her skin was not snow-white, as she had feared, but more a soft gold, like aged ivory. It was stretched tight over her bones, almost too tight around the eyes, giving them a slight upward slant. Her eyes weren't brown nor green nor blue, but were flecked with many colors. Her nose was straight, but not unusually wide, except when she flared her nostrils, which she did when she was provoked. Her lips were full and soft. Her most distinguishing characteristic was a cleft in her chin, which neither her mother nor Master Pearson had, unless it was hidden under the growth of whiskers on his chin that he kept neatly trimmed down to a sharp point.

She took the ribbon from her hair and held it between her teeth. The hair was tangled in knots, and she worked at it until the comb ran easily through it. It was chestnut colored with streaks of red, and it hung down the middle of her back in waves the size of her fingers and as close together.

She divided her hair into three strands and began to weave them together. She could not see what she was doing, so she closed her eyes and used her hands for vision. The first attempt left a snaking snarl down her back, so she tried again. The next time the column of hair felt fairly neat, but clumps that had not been caught in the braid fell teasingly around her face. By this time her arms were crying out in pain. She grunted with frustration and shook them until the blood was circulating again. Isaac offered assistance, but Bea told him that he would not be there to fix her hair every time it needed doing. Franklin said it couldn't be any harder than braiding rope, which he had done hundreds of times, but he did not volunteer to help. She tried once more, and this time she thought she had it. She told George to come over and hold the bottom of her hair while she tied it. George made a move toward Charity, but Bea glared at him, and he backed away again. She pulled the braid over her shoulder, pinched the end in her left hand, took the ribbon from her teeth with her right and tied it tightly. She looked into the mirror once more and determined that it was not a bad job at all.

Charity took the scarf and wrapped it around her neck, then put on her coat. She put the hat on her head and tied it under her chin. Finally, she looked into the mirror once again. It was true— it was hard to tell what race she was. She could have been from Spain or Italy or anywhere.

"Where are you going?" said Bea.

"I'm going to school," said Charity.

"You're going where, girl?" said Franklin.

"I have to get Sissy. I have to tell her about Tess. I'll be back as soon as we say good-bye."

"You heard what the reverend said, Charity," said Bea. "You'll get us all sent back if Hendrick sees you."

"He's looking for two black girls in hiding, Bea," said Charity, "not a light-skinned one at Sissy's school. I won't be gone long."

Charity knew that it was risky to go out, especially without Sissy, but she couldn't let her friend down. She also felt that the risk was hers alone. Whatever Hendrick might do to her, she thought with naive confidence, she wouldn't betray her fellow fugitives. Nothing could be worse than living with herself if Bea, George, or any of the others was recaptured because of something she said or did.

When she went to the door panel, Franklin stood in front of it.

"You being able to come and go like you please," he said, "it don't set right with me. Just because you got a hat don't make you white."

"I never said it did," Charity snapped. Franklin glared at her and then jerked away, and Charity left without looking back.

It was a cold, gray day with a drizzling mist in the air. Mr. Sheffield was no longer lurking in front of the house. Mr. Bigelow must have told him that Sunday was beyond his reach.

Union School was on the corner of College and Willard streets. Charity had never been in a school before, but she had already broken so many of society's rules that she was hardly daunted. She took a deep breath and pulled open the heavy oak door.

Inside a wide hallway echoed the thud of the door closing behind her. The wood floors were marked with water spots from wet boots tromping on them. Sissy had said Miss Joy's room was on the third floor, so she found the stairway and began climbing the steps. The banister had been rubbed smooth by students climbing or descending the stairs, and perhaps, thought Charity, an occasional ride down when the precept was not looking.

On the third floor she faced the task of determining which room was Miss Joy's. She pictured her as rather angelic, in spite of Sissy's description. The doors to the classrooms had windows in them so Charity could see in. She eliminated the rooms that had men standing at the front and narrowed the choice down to three. One classroom had younger children in it, leaving two to choose from. In one was a teacher who had a nose so thin and long that Charity thought she must have to hold the end of it up in order to eat. She had thick, dark eyebrows that grew together over her nose, and her mouth was pinched into a tight little bow. Her lace collar would have come up under her chin, had she had one, and it was girded by ribbon, which Charity was sure was too tight, since her face was crimson. She was delivering a tirade to the class, and her voice penetrated the closed door. Charity decided to see what the other room offered.

Through the window she could see four rows with five desks in each. They were all painted green, and each had its own inkwell in the right-hand corner. The teacher's desk and chair sat on a platform at the front of the room. Behind it on the wall were half-size flags of the American states, and below each was its motto. A boy was standing beside the teacher's desk, facing the classroom. His hands were clasped behind his back, and he appeared to be addressing the students, even though he was staring at a spot on the wall where it met the ceiling. His mouth was open, but his lips were not moving, which indicated that probably nothing was coming from it. The teacher stood on the opposite side of the room in front of a wall of windows. She was a kind-looking, gray-haired woman. In her left hand she held a blackboard pointer with which she tapped the palm of her right hand impatiently.

Smack in the center of the room sat Sissy. She looked none the worse for wear after her Sunday afternoon dip in the lake, and Charity was happy to see that her cheeks were rosy and her hair still had its flame. Sissy did not see Charity. She was looking out the window and stifling a yawn.

Charity knocked firmly, three quick raps. The blackboard pointer paused in midair, and the heads of all the children turned toward the door. The boy at the front of the room sighed in relief and raised his eyes toward heaven. The teacher shook her head and marched across the room in front of the boy, who now assumed a more relaxed posture.

Miss Joy opened the door. "Yes, what is it?" she said curtly.

"I must see Cecilia Young immediately," said Charity.

"Who are you?" said Miss Joy. "I don't remember ever seeing you here before."

"I am . . . " Charity hesitated here. She knew she had to come up with a good one and wished she had practiced on her way to the school. " . . . a friend of Cecilia Young's. Her father asked me to fetch her. There is a family emergency."

"Emergency? What emergency?" asked Miss Joy.

"I'm not at liberty to say," said Charity. "But it has to do with her uncle, who has fallen into some trouble with . . .." Charity let her words trail off.

Miss Joy's eyes narrowed, and she looked at Charity suspiciously. Charity smiled at her with a look of feigned innocence. "What is your name, dear?" asked Miss Joy.

"Helen," said Charity.

"Do you have a last name . . . Helen?"

"Helen Hastings," said Charity without blinking.

"Well, your name has a nice alliterative lilt, Helen. Please come in a moment."

"But I really must see Cecilia. Time is of the utmost."

"I'm sure. But first, I think the class would like to know . . . " Here she waved her hand across the room and spoke so that all the students could hear. ". . . why you are not in school today."

"My school is in New Hampshire, and we are having our spring recess this week."

"I see." Miss Joy looked Charity over carefully. "Well . . . Helen, is it? . . . if you can prove to me that you are, indeed, schooled, then I will believe you and you may take Cecilia for her . . . emergency." Charity looked at Sissy. She was holding up an open book, which covered her nose and mouth. Charity thought she must have been enjoying the drama. "Let me get you a book." She turned toward her desk.

"*Fatti maschii, parole femine,*" said Charity.

"I beg you pardon?" said Miss Joy.

"Manly deeds, womanly words," said Charity. Miss Joy looked puzzled. "The motto for Maryland," she said. Miss Joy twisted her head to look at the wall where the flags were tacked.

"*Esse quam videri*—To be rather than to seem—North Carolina," said Charity. "*Ense petit placidam sub ligertate*—By the sword we seek peace, but peace only under liberty—Massachusetts."

Charity relished the look of surprise on Miss Joy's face. It spurred her on. "*Dum spiro spero*—While I breathe, I hope—South Carolina."

"That's fine," Miss Joy managed to say. "I think you've proven your point."

"*Sic semper tyrannis,*" said Charity, glaring at Miss Joy in the eye. "Thus always to tyrants—Virginia."

"That's quite enough," said Miss Joy.

"No, it is not," said Charity. "One more. The motto of my home state, New Hampshire. Live free or die." She turned to the class. "Let's go, Sissy."

Chapter Twenty-One

Once they were outside the school, Charity told Sissy about Nate going to Canada and Tess packing to leave. Sissy refused to believe it was true and said she had to hear it directly from Tess.

It took Tess a few minutes to answer their knock. Her eyes were swollen, and it was apparent that she had been crying. It was the first time she had seen Sissy since she helped deliver her home soaking wet on Sunday afternoon. She grabbed Sissy and held her tight, her eyes closed and her lips drawn in between her teeth to keep them from trembling. Then she brought the girls inside. Lida was sleeping, she said. The house was littered with clothing and items waiting to be packed.

In the kitchen Tess had been wrapping dishes from the cupboards. A pile of old newspapers was on the table, and Sissy took cups from the shelves and began wrapping sheets of newspaper around them. Charity worked on the plates. Sissy kept pausing to wipe the tears from her cheeks and mop her nose with the back of her hand. Wherever she touched her face, she left a gray smudge from the newsprint. Had she not been so sad, she would have looked comical. Tess did not say much, burying her thoughts in the packing. Charity tried to think of something to say that would be a comfort to them both.

"You should probably just work on what you'll take with you on the train," said Charity. "Sissy and the others can finish packing the rest to ship later."

"I've already put some things in a bag," said Tess. "I just need to gather some snacks and toys for Lida." She picked up a blue pitcher and turned it over in her hands. "Some of these things I just need to handle one more time. You never know what might happen."

"Mr. Bigelow will make sure they get there safe and sound," said Charity.

"Yes, I know he will," said Tess. "I just hope we do."

"Isaac is going with you," said Charity. "He'll see after you."

"Who's Isaac?" said Tess. Charity told her about Isaac and how he had cared for George. He likes children, she explained, and would be helpful with Lida as well as the baggage.

"Why don't you come, Charity?" asked Tess. "Lida has grown fond of you, and you're on your way north anyway."

"I can't leave Bea," said Charity. "And, well, there are some complications."

"Is something keeping you from getting to Canada?" asked Tess.

"More like someone."

"You mean those damned slave catchers are after you, too?" asked Tess, a sharpness in her voice Charity had not heard before.

"It's not just that," said Charity. "It's Franklin. He's convinced Bea that we should go to Africa with him."

"Franklin who?" said Sissy.

125

"Franklin Boggs. He came to the ell several days ago. He wants to go to Liberia."

"Bring Bea to our house," said Sissy.

"She won't go," said Charity.

"Then leave her with Franklin," said Sissy. "You can't spend the rest of your life with your sister, anyway. Let her go to Africa if she wants to."

"You don't understand," said Charity. "Bea is pregnant."

"Lord, Lord, Lord," said Tess. "How far along is she?"

"Well, I don't know," said Charity. "Not far, I don't think."

"Women in her condition sometimes don't know what they're saying," said Tess. "I nearly drove Nate insane the first three months I carried Lida. But she shouldn't be going off to Africa. Can't you convince her to have the baby in Canada?"

"The more you argue with Bea, the less good it does," said Charity.

"I'll have my father talk to Mr. Bigelow, Charity," said Sissy. "They'll know what to do. Maybe they can get you and Bea to Canada right away, before Franklin's plans are set."

"Maybe," said Charity. But she had an unsettling feeling about it all.

"You and Bea can meet up with Nate and Tess in Canada," said Sissy. "Maybe you can even be neighbors."

"And you can come up on summer vacations and stay with us, Sissy," said Tess. "You can be Lida's governess."

"I'd like that, Tess," said Sissy. "It won't be long before school's out."

Charity said nothing. She picked up a plate that was bordered by a silver line. On it was painted a picture of a young couple. Vines grew gracefully around them, and a full moon framed their faces. They looked lovingly into each other's eyes. Below the picture was printed the words, "Be of good cheer!

126

For if we love one another, nothing, in truth, can harm us, whatever mischances may happen!"

"Tess!" said Charity. "Look! This quote is from *Evangeline*. That's one of the books you gave me to read, Sissy."

"It is?" said Sissy.

"Sissy gave that plate to Nate and me as a wedding present. Remember, Sissy?"

"Oh, yes," said Sissy. "Now I remember. Um, I never really read *Evangeline*. What was it about?"

"Evangeline loves Gabriel, the blacksmith's son," said Charity. "They lived in Nova Scotia until the British came and took everything they owned, made them prisoners, and burned their houses. Most of them escaped on ships, but Evangeline and Gabriel got separated. She spent the rest of her life trying to find him."

"Oh, no," said Tess. She grabbed the edge of the table and sat down.

"But it has a happy ending," said Charity. "They find each other at the end." She didn't tell Tess that Gabriel was an old man on his deathbed before Evangeline found him. She wished the plate had a quote from a happier story.

Sissy said she needed to get back to school. She had missed the day before and was behind in mathematics, which was a hard subject for her. But she wanted to see Lida first, and Tess told her to go to the crib because it was time for her to get up anyway. Sissy went into the bedroom to kiss Lida good-bye. In the crib with Lida was a handkerchief doll, its arms and legs made from tying string where the wrists and ankles would be.

"Look, Charity," said Sissy. "I made this doll for Lida a few weeks ago. I told her she could take it to church because it wouldn't make any noise if she dropped it. We called it her Sunday doll." Sissy rubbed Lida's back, and the little girl raised a sleepy head.

"Sis-sis," she said, sitting up. When she saw Charity, she held out her arms toward her. Charity smiled and picked her up, and Lida tried to poke a finger into her eye. Then Lida twisted around and reached out for Sissy.

"Happen?" said Lida, pointing to the smudges on Sissy's cheeks, her eyes wide. Sissy looked at Charity.

"She must think you got bruised falling through the ice," said Charity, and they laughed.

"Now, you be a good girl," said Sissy, "and don't give your mother a hard time." She gave Lida a bear hug and then gave her back to Tess. Sissy hugged Tess with Lida sandwiched between them, which brought giggles from Lida.

Charity did not say good-bye to Tess and Lida. She would be sure to find them in Montreal—it couldn't be such a big place. And Isaac and Sunday would be there, too. She was looking forward to getting there, settling down with Bea before spring came. Bea would like Tess, and Lida would have a little playmate before too long. Charity wanted it to work out, in spite of the nagging feeling that it might not.

Charity and Sissy started up the street. At the corner, Charity looked back to see Tess still standing in the doorway holding Lida, whose little fist opened and closed in good-bye. Sissy put her arm through Charity's, and they walked on in silence for a while.

"It's just not going to be the same around here. I wish you could stay and keep me company, Charity," said Sissy. "Hey, why don't you come back to school with me? There must be something you haven't learned."

"No, thanks. I've had about all the Joy I can handle for one day." Charity glanced to see if there was a reaction to her pun, but Sissy was no longer beside her. She turned and saw Sissy staring up the walk.

"Don't look now, but there's that fat man we saw at the

hotel," she said. Leaning against Edward Peck's store was Hendrick, cigar stump wedged between his teeth and one hand on the curve of his cane handle. He was watching people pass, nodding at anyone who met his gaze. He looked down the street just as Charity turned to run. Sissy took hold of her jacket and stopped her.

"It's too late. He's seen us," she said. "We just have to pretend nothing's the matter. Stick right by me. It'll be okay." Charity had no choice. She matched Sissy's pace up the walk.

When they neared Hendrick, Charity could feel herself trembling.

"Afternoon, ladies," he said, drawling the words. His voice froze her spine and made her legs numb. The girls kept walking. "You two playing hooky from school today?"

"We're on our way back from lunch, sir," said Sissy. She had slowed down to speak to him.

"You the ones Willy Peck was talking about?"

Sissy halted and turned toward him. "I thought Willy Peck wasn't able to talk," she said.

"Yeah, but the boy's literate, and there's nothing wrong with his writing hand." He must have written the whole story out. Charity looked around for an escape, but there was nowhere to hide.

"You the girl who fell through the ice?" He was speaking to Sissy. Now even she did not have a retort. Charity peeked up at him from under the brow of her hat. If she could see his eyes, she might be able to determine how much he knew. But she had to be careful, very careful, of every move. The smell of cigar nauseated her, and she swallowed hard to force back the bile that was rising in her throat.

"This one looks like she's been in a tussle with that hand." Charity covered the bandage on her right hand with her left. "What's the matter with you, gal, you tongue-tied?" The cigar stub wiggled in his mouth when he talked, as if it were alive. When he smiled, his brown teeth showed and his eyes disappeared into layers of flesh.

"Willy seems to think you might know where I can find a couple of Negro girls I'm looking for. I suspect they're hiding in town here somewheres. I'm not about to leave until I find them, either." He took the cigar from his mouth and spat a brown glob onto the walkway. Sissy and Charity both took a step back.

"After a while I just might lose my patience and take me a couple of white girls instead. You two'd do pretty well." A laugh gurgled from his throat. "Or maybe you're not white at all. Let me have a good look at this one." He reached down to lift the brim of the bonnet, but Sissy jumped between them and batted his hand away, kicking him in the shin at the same time. As Hendrick reached to grab his wounded leg, Sissy's foot came up between his legs. The hard boot toe hit home, and he fell to his knees.

Charity edged away from Sissy and Hendrick and tried to make herself inconspicuous against the front wall of a store. Sissy screamed, "Help! Take your hands off me! Help!" Edward Peck ran out of his store and knocked Hendrick onto his side on the boardwalk. People began to crowd around the conflict, ignoring Charity, and she forced herself to walk slowly and casually until she rounded the corner and left Church Street behind. Hendrick, it seemed, was temporarily silenced by his pain, and no one followed her. Charity felt shaky and sick, but she kept moving—the ell was not far away.

Chapter Twenty-Two

Charity's boots squished in the mud behind the ell. The air smelled of earth, fertile and about to spring to life. She wondered why people up north look so forward to springtime. Nature comes alive, it's true, but from what she'd heard, the birthing process wasn't all that pleasant. Downright painful, even. It was dying that was easy. You just let go, that's all. No struggle, no pain. It must be like going to sleep. And the time in between being born and dying, well, that was a struggle, too. The only thing that made it all worth the effort was the peace at the end of it. She didn't like thinking these thoughts, but she felt like life was closing in on her. Just like the sticky blossoms that were forming on the bushes, she knew something was about to burst open.

A gust of wind blew against her, and Charity reached up to hold the bonnet against its force. Her hand waved vainly above her head. The bonnet was gone. She turned around to see if it was hanging down her back. She felt at her neck for the sashes and looked around her feet. No bonnet. It was a sign, she told herself. The bonnet had served its purpose, whether for good or evil. Now she was on her own.

Charity hoped no one saw her enter the ell. She was afraid to look around, afraid she'd look suspicious. Once inside, she kept the events of the day to herself. She didn't want to alarm Bea, and maybe by not talking about it she could pretend it didn't even happen. Still, Hendrick stuck in her mind like a tick, feeding on her and growing bigger by the minute.

When Mr. Bigelow came for Isaac that night, he said that two more fugitives were on their way to the ell. They were both men, he said, and perhaps Bea and Charity would be more comfortable at Reverend Young's house. Sissy had apparently gotten her father to talk to Mr. Bigelow.

"Let me make one thing clear," said Bea. "When I leave this place, I'm going straight to freedom, and I'm not making any more stops along the way."

"Of course, it's your decision," said Mr. Bigelow. Charity wished he wouldn't give up so easily. "I expect the new arrivals will get here sometime before morning. You'd best make a space for them to sleep."

"What do you know about them?" asked Franklin. His wound was much better. His shoulder was still bandaged, but he was putting a shirt on over it as he spoke. He moved his arm without wincing with pain.

"One of them is fair-skinned," said Mr. Bigelow. "He has been passing himself off as a white man traveling with his gentleman servant. They've come all the way from South Carolina without so much as a raised eyebrow."

"Anybody trailing them?" said Franklin.

"Not that I've heard," said Mr. Bigelow.

"There's plenty of room for all of us here," said Bea. Her word was final.

When Isaac left with Mr. Bigelow, George was asleep. Isaac

left a note by his bed and told Charity not to read it to him, but to teach him until he was able to read it himself. Then he embraced each of them, including Franklin.

"Take care of yourself," he told Charity. "And watch over your sister, too."

"I will," said Charity. It seemed as if she was always saying good-bye. The only thing she had been able to hold onto the last few months was Bea. Somehow she had to make sure she didn't lose her.

When Mr. Bigelow brought the new visitors shortly before daybreak, Charity got up and lighted some lamps. Bea was already up, looking over the medical supplies in case the men needed tending.

The first man was about thirty years old and wore a neatly tailored suit of clothes, but his head was bare. He was almost as big as Franklin and beamed with energy. The second man was slight and frail. His clothes were too large for him, and he looked shriveled up inside them. His right arm rested in a sling inside the jacket, and the coat sleeve hung limp at his side. A strip of linen was tied around his face as if his jaw were injured. A tall hat was pulled down over the bandage, and it covered the tops of his ears. Charity could not see his eyes because he wore dark green glasses. He was so pale that Charity thought at first he was a white man. Franklin eyed him cautiously. Mr. Bigelow introduced them as Harry Walker and Bill Jones, then left, saying he had to get the wagon off the street before sun-up.

"Make yourselves comfortable," said Charity. "We'll make up a pot of coffee."

Bill, the large man, took his coat off and then began helping Harry. First, off came the hat. Harry's hair was cropped short all over his head. Next, Bill removed the linen from around Harry's head.

"Do you have a toothache?" asked Charity. "Bea might have some clove oil that will help."

"Naw," said Bill. "We figured the less this white face showed, the less folks would be able to judge Harry's real color." Harry smiled oddly, as if he had a secret that was tickling him. He removed his dark glasses with his left hand. His face was delicate, with angular cheeks and a narrow chin. His thin eyebrows and long lashes made him look almost pretty.

Bill removed Harry's jacket and untied the sling from around his neck. "Is your arm hurt?" asked Charity.

"No," said Harry. "But I don't know how to write, so when we stayed in hotels, I just told them my arm was sprained, or sometimes I said it was a bad case of arthritis. That way, we didn't have to sign in."

Once the sling was off, Charity noticed that Harry had lumps inside his shirt where breasts would have been if he had been a woman. She thought it odd, but did not mention it. "You must be tired," she said. "Why don't you sit down and have a rest."

"I'm not worn out at all," said Harry. "In fact, I'm so glad to be here, I could dance a jig." Harry began to hop around the room in a little dance step, and Charity saw that the lumps were bouncing up and down the way breasts do. Bill saw that Charity was staring at Harry's chest.

"I guess I better introduce my wife to you all. This is Ellen Craft, and my name is William Craft." Ellen smiled, and Franklin burst into a throaty laugh. Bea and Charity joined in, and they all laughed until their stomachs hurt.

George woke up. "What's going on?" he said.

"George," said Charity. "Meet Ellen Craft and her husband, William."

"Something funny about their names?" said George. And they all began to laugh again.

Bea poured the coffee, and they sat down to talk.

"How did you manage to pull off the disguise?" asked Charity.

"We told people that Ellen was a sickly planter on his way to Philadelphia for medical treatment," said William. "That way they let me ride in the same train car to wait on her."

"People were sympathetic," said Ellen. "Everyone wanted to help. Sometimes I had trouble keeping a straight face."

"We stayed in only the best hotels on the way," said William. "I guessed that would be the last place slave hunters would expect to find runaways."

"Yes, sir," said Ellen. "Came first class the whole way. Still, sometimes I was a nervous wreck."

"When we get up north, I think we should get us a couple of jobs acting on the stage. Right, honey?" said William.

"I'm not acting like anybody but my own sweet self from now on," said Ellen. "But I'll throw flowers on the stage at you if that's what you really want to do, William." They all broke into laughter once more.

"Where did you get the money to stay in fancy hotels?" asked Franklin.

"Well," said William, "to put it to you truthfully, I had me a little cotton business going."

"You stole cotton from the master and sold it?" said Franklin. "You could get yourself killed for doing a crazy thing like that."

"I wouldn't rightly call it stealing," said William. "Way I figure it is like this. I belonged to the master, right?"

"Yeah," said Franklin.

"And the cotton belonged to the master. You with me?"

"So?"

"That makes me and the cotton kind of like brothers, see? And brothers, they got to watch out for each other. So making the money was just a brotherly act on the part of the cotton." William grinned at Franklin. "And I thank him kindly for it."

"If you don't beat anything I ever saw," said Franklin, shaking his head. "Here I am sleeping in swamps with snakes swimming around my head and leeches sucking at my legs, and you staying in first-class hotels just because you got a white woman with you."

"You watch yourself," said William. "You about to step over the line of good taste."

"What do you know about good taste?" said Franklin. "You seem to forget you're a slave, just like me."

"Not anymore, I'm not."

Franklin was quiet for a minute. "I don't like this idea of passing yourself off as white. That makes you just as bad as they are. And now we got two white women we got to deal with."

"Franklin, that's enough," said Bea. "Don't be like them and judge people by what color their skin is."

Franklin looked at her, but he didn't say anything. He packed tobacco into his pipe and lit it. He looked at Bea as he drew in the smoke and watched her through the cloud he blew out.

William spoke next. "I guess we made fools of some white folks, but what we did was nothing compared to some of the others I heard about."

"Like who?" said George.

"Well, let me tell you about Henry Box Brown," said William. "Ever hear of him?" George shook his head. "He was a slave in Virginia. Pretty handy with a hammer and saw, too. He made a big box for himself and then got a white friend, a shoe dealer, to nail him inside and mail him up north. His friend sent the box to someone on the Vigilance Committee in Philadelphia and got word to him to expect a delivery on the three o'clock morning train from the south. When the box got there, a bunch of Vigilance Committee members were waiting for it. They suspected somebody was inside, but they were afraid to open it because they thought he might be dead. They knocked on the lid, and Henry said, 'All right, sir.' So they opened it up with a saw and hatchet, and Henry popped out just like a jack-in-the-box and said, 'How do you do, gentlemen.'" George giggled convulsively, holding his sides, and Charity snickered.

"How come nobody else tried it after that?" asked George.

"They did," said William. "But they got caught. In fact, the shoe dealer ended up spending eight years in jail for his part in it."

"Then there was Harriet Jacobs," said Ellen. "She spent seven years in a crawlspace over a shed waiting for a chance to escape. Her master thought she had run up north and sent men to Massachusetts to look for her. Meantime, she was holed up in a space so small she couldn't sit up straight. It was freezing in the winter and roasting in the summer. And bugs? Um-um," she said, shaking her head.

"What happened to her?" asked Charity.

"She had two children, and she watched them through a knothole those seven years. They didn't even know she was there. Only one who did was her grandmother, who pushed food up to her and took her waste pot down every day. Finally, her grandmother got word to a neighbor about Harriet. He was so amazed at what she'd been through, he said she deserved to be set free. He helped her escape with her children."

Charity was right about Ellen being pretty. In fact, she was beautiful. Charity liked the way Ellen's hands drew pictures

137

in the air when she told the story, the way her eyes sparkled and the sweet tone of her voice when she talked about Harriet Jacobs. Harriet must have been a devoted mother to want to stay close to her children in spite of what she had to go through. Like Tess was with Lida. Charity wished she had someone who loved her that much. She could hardly remember her own mother. She looked at Bea, who was sewing the hem of her old skirt. Bea was right—it was time for Charity to learn to take care of herself. Bea might not always be there to lead her on whatever journey she had to take. She'd have to find her own way alone one day, perhaps sooner than she'd like.

"There are a lot more stories," said William, "and we could be here all day telling them."

"We'll probably be here all day anyway," said George.

William laughed. "I guess you're right about that, boy." He rubbed George's head playfully.

"You hear any war talk on your way up?" asked Franklin.

"Things are heating up down in South Carolina," said William. "They're talking secession."

"What's secession?" said George.

"Withdrawing from the United States on account of slavery," said Ellen. "And if that happens, hang on. Things are going to bust loose."

"I'm going to be busting loose myself before that happens," said Franklin.

"If war comes, I may be coming back to fight for the north," said William. "Defeating the south looks like the only way we're going to end slavery and be allowed to go back where we came from."

"That's exactly where I'm going," said Franklin. "Back to Africa. Liberia."

"You don't mean that," said William. "You're an American."

"I don't feel pride in calling myself that," said Franklin. "America is a white man's country."

"Don't fool yourself," said William. His tone was not antagonistic; he seemed to know that Franklin was not one to argue with. "Liberia is a white man's country, too. He made it, he supports it, sends supplies over, and makes the decisions about what happens with it. He may not show his face often, but he's there just the same."

"If I stay here, there's always the chance somebody's going to try to own me again," said Franklin. "I'm not going to let that happen. Bea's going with me. Little sister, too. And George can come if he wants." There was a tense silence. Charity tapped her fingers on the table. William cleared his throat.

"Maybe I'll have me another cup of coffee," said Ellen.

Chapter Twenty-Three

William and Ellen settled into the cellar room. Charity liked having them around, and the uneasy feeling she had earlier started to dissolve. William took a particular liking to George.

"Ever play bowls, George?" he asked.

"No, sir," said George.

"Let me show you how it's done," said William. "We take this stone, see, and toss it over by the wall. Now, you get two small stones, and I get two small stones. See how close you can throw your stones to that first one. If I get closer than you, I win the round. We'll play five rounds. Ready?" After five rounds, Charity asked if she could play, too, and the three of them passed the time quickly. William scratched a crisscross board into the floor, and they played with chestnuts and acorns. Then William taught George how to whittle a top out of wood. It didn't spin well at first, but William made a few adjustments, and it danced across the floor.

After a while, William said, "Well, George, who's going to meet you up in the Promised Land?"

"Don't know," said George. "Nobody, I guess."

"You mean you don't have no folks at all?" said William.

"No," said George, and he picked at an invisible mole on his arm.

"Ellen, did you hear that?" said William. "This boy's got nowhere to go when he gets up north."

"Well now, that's a problem," said Ellen. "Or is it? We're going get ourselves a big house, and there'll be a lot of room. Would you like to come with us on the last leg of our journey, George?" George nodded eagerly. Ellen smiled at him, then to Charity added, "I'd like it if you came too."

Charity did not answer. She needed to get Bea alone to try to make her forget about going to Africa. She still held onto the dream of a home with Bea and the baby. Ellen seemed to read her mind, and she changed the subject.

"You sure do have pretty hair, Charity." Ellen came over to Charity and stroked her braid. "My hair was long like yours." Her hand went toward her own head but stopped at her shoulder, and she looked across the room at William, who was playing with George. She lifted Charity's hair and untied the ribbon at the end of the braid.

"If you've got a comb, I'll show you how all the ladies in Boston were wearing their hair when we came through."

Bea gave Ellen a warning look, but Ellen ignored her. Charity got Sunday's comb, and Ellen untangled the strands and made a part down the center of Charity's head. Then she wove two braids and wound them around Charity's ears, tucking in the ends with hairpins from her coat pocket. When Charity saw herself in the hand mirror, she thought she looked just like a picture in one of Bethy's issues of Godey's Lady's Book.

Ellen stood back and crossed her arms. She was the color of beach sand, and her eyes were as green as emeralds. She noticed Charity inspecting her, and after a minute she came closer and said, almost in a whisper, "A lot of us are light-skinned. It makes the white man hate us even more. But it's a two-edged knife. The black man doesn't want us around either, because we remind him of his master." She patted the coils on the sides of Charity's head and adjusted the pins. "Sometimes I feel like I just don't belong any place."

It hadn't occurred to Charity that someone else might feel the way she did. It comforted her to know that others shared her problem. Maybe she wasn't so strange after all.

"What about William?" asked Charity. His love for Ellen shone in his face whenever he looked at her.

"Some people, the good ones, look right past your skin and see what's in your heart," said Ellen. "William's one of them. There are others out there too, like Mr. and Mrs. Bigelow. You look hard enough, you'll find them."

Charity told Ellen about the black bonnet and Sissy, and passing herself off as Marie in Burlington. Ellen agreed that she was clever, but warned her about the danger she put herself in every time she left the hiding place. "It sounds like you better sit tight from now on," she said.

A knock banged heavily on the wall panel. Franklin pushed it open, and Mrs. Bigelow's worried face appeared from the shadow.

"There's trouble," she said, wringing her hands. "That slave hunter, Hendrick, is on his way here with Sheriff Barnes and some other men. Sheriff Barnes has a warrant to search the house. Lucius is getting a wagon ready. You'd better start through the tunnel right away. I'll try to stall them." Then she disappeared.

William grabbed a jacket and handed it to George.

"Come on, son," he said and pushed George toward the opening to the tunnel. "We'll be right behind you. Let's go, Ellen."

"Charity, get your coat," said Ellen. Charity looked at Bea.

"You can't tell me that six Negroes in a carriage won't attract attention," said Franklin. "If we can make it to the river, we can head east toward New Hampshire. They'll be looking for us up north."

"I'm going with Franklin," Bea said.

"Bea, no!" said Charity, and she grabbed her sister's arm. Bea jerked loose from Charity's grip.

"You go with Ellen and William, sister," Bea said.

Footsteps thundered up the stairs. "Bea, they're going up to the attic. When they see we're not there, they'll come down here," said Charity.

"We have to leave—now," said William. He took Ellen's hand and helped her into the opening. "I'll see to the girl," he told her. Charity looked at Ellen, whose eyes pleaded for her to follow. William put a hand on Charity's shoulder. "It's time," he said.

"Bea, please," said Charity.

Bea cupped Charity's face in her hands. "I been trying to make you see that you're a woman now, sister," she said. "You got to take care of things by yourself. And I got to do what's right for me. You go on, now. And remember what Sunday said about not looking back."

Charity threw her arms around Bea's neck and pressed her cheek against her sister's. "I love you, Bea," she said. Then she turned and crawled through the tunnel. The cold blackness wrapped its frozen fingers around her bones. She inched forward, fighting the shiver that shook her and fighting the urge to turn around and pull Bea along with her. When she saw the light ahead at last, it was dim and blurry.

I can't cry now, she told herself, but the tears kept coming.

Chapter Twenty-Four

§

Charity ran her fingers along the coarse twine tied around the brown package. Tess said it had come in the middle of April from Burlington, but it had taken her weeks to track Charity down. She had been tempted to open it, in case it contained something that could spoil, but it was addressed to Charity, and she didn't want to pry. Whoever sent it knew that Tess was in Montreal and that she would eventually find Charity.

Now it was May. William was working for the railroad company, and Ellen had her hands full getting the house settled and taking care of George. Charity was teaching him every day, and his reading was progressing. Ellen sat in on his lessons, and already she could write the alphabet and read the labels on the canned goods at the store. Charity had her own room with a bed by the window so she could feel the morning sun wash over her, and she could lean out and smell the lilacs and hear the mourning doves. Her life was all she had hoped, except that she still hadn't heard from Bea. She hoped the package held good news, but her instincts told her it didn't.

She took a pair of scissors off Ellen's desk and cut the twine. She tore the paper away from a flat box, lifted the lid, and pulled back the tissue paper inside to reveal the bonnet. The black satin was faded to dark gray and splotched with stains. The brim was ripped, and the whole hat was misshapen. The flower that had been on top was gone, and only one sash remained. It was a useless old thing, but Charity smiled when she held it up. The bonnet smelled like lavender, and Sissy's face flashed across her memory.

Beneath the bonnet was an envelope addressed to her. Her hands shook as she opened it. It read:

March 24, 1858

Dear Charity,

I hope you are happy in your new home. I don't know if you've heard about what happened to Bea, so I guess I'd better tell you. My father got the word from Sheriff Barnes. After you left for St. Albans, Franklin and Bea took off running, and some deputies jumped onto the police wagon and followed them. They ran into some thick woods, but the briars kept snagging on Bea's skirt, and she couldn't keep up with Franklin, so he carried her. They had just reached the Winooski River when Sheriff Barnes and his men caught up with them. They had to leave the wagon behind on the road, and Hendrick couldn't keep up because of his bad leg. Sheriff Barnes threatened to shoot Franklin if he didn't put Bea down, but he just ran into the water with Bea in his arms. The sheriff shot to wound him, but he missed his aim and hit Bea. Franklin wailed like a wild man. When they got to him, it took three of them to drag him from the river and get the chains on his hands and feet. Hendrick was as mad as the devil when he caught up and said his boss was going to throttle him for losing both of you.

We buried Bea in the graveyard by our church. When you come back, I'll take you up to put flowers on her grave. She'd like that.

Willy Peck is all better, and he's working in his father's store again. I guess he can talk all right, but he doesn't talk to me anymore, and I'm not complaining about that.

It will be spring soon, and come summer I'll get myself up to Canada to see you and Tess and Nate and Lida. Give them my love, will you? And save some for you, too.

Love,

Sissy

P.S. Here's that old black bonnet. I found it in the mud not far from Mr. Bigelow's house. I cleaned it up as best I could. I know you don't need it anymore, but I thought you might like to have it.

Charity folded the letter again and put it back into the envelope, but the message echoed through her like the sound of the rifle shot that night not so long ago, even though it seemed like a lifetime. Bea's death left a hollow feeling that would take a long time to fill, if ever, but Ellen and William and George would take up some of the emptiness as, day by day, they became her new family.

Sunday said not to look back, but there was one piece of old business Charity had to take care of before she could get on with her new life. She put the bonnet aside and opened a drawer of Ellen's desk. She took out a piece of paper, inked the pen in the well, and began to write:

May 16, 1858

Miss Elizabeth Pearson
Primrose Plantation
Roanoke, Virginia

Dear Bethy,

I am writing to you from the city of Montreal in Quebec, Canada. It took me a long time to reach freedom, and many things have happened along the way. Bea died. She was trying to escape to Africa, but the slave hunters caught her. I miss her very much. I thought she was my only sister, but she told me that I have another sister who is still in Virginia. You may know her. I hope some day she and I can meet up with each other and be friends.

I live with a nice couple, and I have a little stepbrother. He is very smart. I have taught him to read, and soon he will read as well as you do. He wants to go back to America some day and graduate from the University of Vermont. But first the matter of slavery will have to be settled. I hear there may be war. If there is, maybe you could come to Canada and stay awhile. If you contact my friend Cecilia Young in Burlington, Vermont, she will come with you.

Spring is finally arriving in the north. I am glad at last to be able to be who I am and say what I think. When I see you again, things will be different between us. Take care of yourself, Bethy.

Sincerely,
Charity Bonnet

Charity addressed the envelope and sealed the letter inside it. She pushed herself away from the desk and walked to the front door. Outside a patch of daffodils swung their yellow trumpets in the warm breeze, and the yard was green with new spring grass. It was a nice day out. Maybe Lida would like to take a walk to the post office.

Afterword

Although the main characters in *The Black Bonnet* are fictional, many of the minor characters are real. Joshua Young was the minister of the Unitarian Church in Burlington until 1859. When he preached the funeral sermon for John Brown after his rebellion at Harpers Ferry, Reverend Young's congregation asked for his resignation, and he moved to Massachusetts. Lucius Bigelow, the editor and publisher of the *Burlington Daily News*, was the chief engineer on the underground railroad in Burlington. Edward Peck, owner of a Burlington dry goods store, and Simon Wires were also conductors on the underground railroad.

Many of the fugitive slaves were also real, although it is not certain that they passed through Burlington on their way to freedom. Among them are William and Ellen Craft and George Henderson, the first black man to graduate from the University of Vermont. The character of Franklin Boggs is based on a real fugitive named Jeremiah Boggs. Other fugitives mentioned in the novel were real as well: Harriet Tubman, Harriet Jacobs, Henry Box Brown, and Sojourner Truth. Many others are nameless, but they loaned me their stories through narratives, legends, and dreams.